A
PUBLIC
SPACE
No. 30

D1597462

The past will reveal to us the nature of
the present. —Joan Perucho

Marcelyn McNeil

No. 30   # TABLE OF CONTENTS

A PUBLIC SPACE
(ISSN 1558-965X;
ISBN 9781733973007)
IS PUBLISHED BY
A PUBLIC SPACE
LITERARY PROJECTS, INC.
PO BOX B, NEW YORK,
NY 10159. PRINTED IN
CANADA.
ISSUE 30, 2021.©2021
A PUBLIC SPACE
LITERARY PROJECTS, INC.
POSTMASTER PLEASE
SEND CHANGES OF
ADDRESS TO A PUBLIC
SPACE, PO BOX B, NEW
YORK, NY 10159.

**A PUBLIC SPACE
IS SUPPORTED
IN PART BY**

The Literary Arts Emergency Fund

**A PUBLIC SPACE IS A
PROUD MEMBER OF**
The Community of
Literary Magazines and
Presses

$[\text{c l m p}]$

No. 30   A PUBLIC SPACE

FOUNDING BENEFACTOR
Deborah Pease
(1943-2014)

BOARD OF DIRECTORS
Charles Buice
Elizabeth Gaffney
Kristen Mitchell
Katherine Bell
Yiyun Li
Robert Sullivan
Brigid Hughes

ADVISORY BOARD
Robert Casper
Fiona McCrae
James Meader
Josh Rolnick

EDITOR
Brigid Hughes

MANAGING EDITOR
Megan Cummins

POETRY EDITOR
Brett Fletcher Lauer

ASSOCIATE EDITORS
Sarah Blakley-Cartwright
Sidik Fofana
Taylor Michael
Laura Preston

COVER DESIGN
Janet Hansen

COPY EDITOR
Anne McPeak

CONTRIBUTING EDITORS
Yiyun Li
Annie Coggan
Martha Cooley
Edwin Frank
Mark Hage
John Haskell
Fiona Maazel
Ayana Mathis
Robert Sullivan
Antoine Wilson

INTERNATIONAL CONTRIBUTING EDITORS
A. N. Devers
(England)
Dorthe Nors
(Denmark)
Natasha Randall
(England)
Motoyuki Shibata
(Japan)

EDITOR AT LARGE
Elizabeth Gaffney

SUBSCRIPTIONS
Postpaid subscription
for 3 issues: $36 in
the United States;
$54 in Canada;
$66 internationally.
Subscribe at
www.apublicspace.org
or send a check to the
address below.

CONTACT
For general queries,
please email
general@apublicspace.org
or call (718) 858-8067.
A Public Space
is located at
PO Box B
New York, NY 10159.

EDITORIAL FELLOW
Miguel Coronado

READERS
Joshua Craig, Julia
Ring, Alex Yeranossian

INTERN
Claire Margot Dauge-Roth

Marcelyn McNeil

TIME KEEPING

MATT MILLER

Time was I knew my place.
Time was there was more to it.
Time was swallowing the children.
Time was an instant, a moment.
Time had all the cards.
Time blistered the cubes.
Time amassed its whistles.
Time had never known better.
Time was cheaply redeemed.
Time organized the birds.
Time tested itself with a shadow.
Time vanished in a disk.
Time had certain commitments.
Time knew the way to the quiet field.
Time never dirtied its fingers.

Marcelyn McNeil

MYSTERIES OF YESTERYEAR
JOAN PERUCHO

Joan Perucho (1920-2003) wrote in both Catalan and Spanish and in most every genre—including art criticism and gastronomical writing—but considered himself a poet above all. He saw his apocryphal stories as a way of installing himself in the heart of the past. "The past will reveal to us the nature of the present," he said. "As for the future, I see no signs that it will be happy."

APPARITIONS AND GHOSTS

It actually wasn't that hard to invoke spirits around a table. They were everywhere. Right there in Paris, in those years, the ghost of Jacques de Molay, the last grand master of the Knights Templar, burned alive in 1314, would regularly show up with no need for summoning and brazenly wind his way around the tip of the Vert-Galant, the Place Dauphine, and along the Pont Neuf. The Cluny museum also had its own bloody spirit, who only appeared to ladies, in the room that held the torture instruments, and in the light of day. That's without taking into account the countless nighttime specters who wandered among the tombs of the Père-Lachaise cemetery reciting their sorrows for all to hear. One of those spirits, a young woman who'd been seduced and abandoned, left a perfumed trail of very fine lace handkerchiefs, sadly soaked with tears.

Things got exciting when Sofia Walder arrived in Paris from Charleston. Following the death of the Luciferian and apostate Abbe Constant, she became the leader of the Freemason occultists. Miss Walder was very beautiful and the favorite disciple of General Albert Pike, creator of the New and Reformed Palladium Rite. She was possessed of a diabolical temper and a glacial gaze and waswell aware of what she was doing. According to Léo Taxil, it was she who came up with the anticlerical version of "La Marseillaise," whose abominable and celebrated first verses were as follows:

Allons! fils de la République,
Le jour du vote est arrivé!
Contre nous de la noire clique
L'oriflamme ignoble est levée (bis).

Entendez-vous tous ces infâmes
Croasser leurs stupides chants?
Ils voudraient, encore, les brigands,
Salir nos enfants et nos femmes.

Miss Walder forced the devil to show up in the flesh. The first time she did it turned out horribly but did serve to cement her lifelong command over him. Doctor Bataille, a very renowned occultist, explains it in his *Le diable au XIXe siècle*: "It happened at the home of Madame X., one Saturday evening, the day consecrated to Moloch. The lovely Sofia Walder had not warned anyone of her aims, and she began to say seven times the name of the Antichrist, which is Apollonius Zabah. She then immediately recited the invocation of Moloch, humbly apologizing for summoning him without the proper tools and pleading with him to appear at the gathering without claiming any victims. Suddenly, the table she was using for the spiritist exercises jumped up toward the ceiling and, as it fell, metamorphosed into a hideous crocodile with bat wings. There was general panic, and everyone was nailed to their seat, petrified. But the surprise reached a climax when the crocodile went over to an upright piano in the room, opened it up, sat down on the bench, and began to play a dissonant melody while directing an expressive and passionate gaze at Madame X., the lady of the house, leaving her modesty unsettled and her sentiments alarmed.

"Finally, the winged crocodile disappeared suddenly, leaving—strangely enough—all the liquor bottles on the buffet empty."

Miss Walder's success made her enormously famous. Yet around that same time, news came from the lodges in Philadelphia about another young woman gifted in the evil arts. Her name was Diana Vaughan and she was also very beautiful, although hers was a seemingly angelic beauty. Diana, one day, made a request at the Paris lodge, using forced relocation as a pretext, and asked to be admitted there. Sofia had a bad feeling about it and convinced the lodge secretary, a man by the name of Bordone, to present a motion against her admittance. They had gathered up the board of directors when, suddenly, a horrific scream was heard. In that exact moment, wicked Bordone's head spun round on his shoulders and stopped when it was facing behind him. Every effort to return his head to its rightful place floundered and, finally, Sofia summoned a *maleach* who told them that the event had been caused by Asmodeus, the protector of Diana Vaughan, and that only she, if she received enough apologies, could bring an end to that highly vexing situation.

The Saint Jacques Triangle, which was the name of the Parisian lodge, sent a telegram ipso facto to Philadelphia with the most flattering compliments. Upon seeing it, Diana announced her immediate departure for Paris, and Bordone remained impatiently awaiting her during the twenty days it took her to cross the Atlantic. The poor wretch lost his appetite and quite a bit of weight, he didn't leave the house, he covered his head with enormous scarves, and anyone asking to see him was told he was away on a trip. When Diana finally arrived, Bordone fell at her feet, begging forgiveness. Diana, who despite everything was good-natured, conceded his wish and, taking his head in her hands, gently returned it to its natural position.

Following those unparalleled occurrences, Sofia Walder's star began to fade. Jealousy ate away at her heart. Diana was constantly gaining ground at the expense of Sofia, her mortal enemy, and replacing her everywhere. Once, Sofia Walder summoned the spirit of Ramon Sibiude, who answered her in Latin, leaving her with some written jottings that read: *"Omnes qui eidem Adamo participavimus atque a serpente in fraudem inducti sumus, per peccatum mortui, ac per coelestem Adamo [um] saluti restituti atque ad vitae lignum…, etc."* In the text he twice used the word *Adamo* when, really, the second time he should have written *Adamum*. Was it possible that Sibiude could make a grammatical error in his Latin? Of course not, Diana triumphantly declared. That was the final straw that irrevocably sunk Sofia Walder.

Diana glimmered with power and beauty, and her reign lasted many years. In the end she converted to Catholicism, repented for her mistakes and, before her death, published a memoir that told all about the Masonic lodges. This "memoir" sold out quickly yet, inexplicably and despite all the time that's passed, has never been reprinted.

No one knows what fate befell Sofia Walder, and her persona was plunged into the very darkest shadows. Some years later, it was said that a group of magicians in Lisbon had cut off her hands, which would gesticulate in response to any questions posed them. Many people searched for these bewitched hands and were willing to offer their weight in gold to obtain them, but they were never found. As the French say, it's a story to make you sleep standing up. Nevertheless, I know of enthusiasts with cold, pallid skin, who still look for them in taxidermy shops, in antique stores and at the ragman's, in museums, and even on the outskirts of large cities, in those empty lots where children play soccer beside construction sites, amid rubble and refuse, the sorts of places where it's possible to find anything and everything: Sofia Walder's hands, the crumpled gray flower of misery, or that one marvelous word that would shatter the world into fifty thousand shards.

HOW BEDEVILING
BE THE DEVILS

When casting spells, warlocks rely on magical circles to protect them when the devils they summon appear. It seems there is nothing at all pleasant about the spectacle, and if they drop their guard even slightly, they get a terrific thrashing, as happened to our compatriot, the magician Belarmino de Arriaza, who was left with a twisted spine as a result of a spell gone wrong. Devils are particularly peeved when they are forced to appear, which is why *The Sworn Book of Honorius* gives detailed instructions on how to draw the circles, adding that one can never safely summon demons without being inside a protective circle, since the first thing they'll do is seize hold of and pummel you.

However, in some cases the demons show up entirely uninvited. One of those cases—perhaps the most peculiar—is that of Monsieur Alexis-Vicent-Charles Berbiguier, who lived at number 54 rue Mazarine in Paris from 1813 to 1817, and suffered indescribably from the devils and imps that followed him everywhere. He would encounter them in his house, on the street, crossing the Pont Neuf and the Pont au Change, and even beneath the portico of the Église Saint-Roch or when visiting at friends' homes. Berbiguier sharpened his ability to see hellish things to such an extent that he was able to discover the devils' representatives here in our world. For example: Moreau, Beelzebub's representative in Paris; Nicolas, a doctor from Avignon and the representative of Moloch; Prieur, a drug merchant and representative of Lilith, etc.

The occultist Émile Grillot de Givry tells us, in his *Le musée des sorciers, mages et alchimistes*, that Vincent-Charles Berbiguier had a nemesis, the warlock M. Pinel, who lived at number 12 rue des Postes. One day, evil Pinel arrived at Berbiguier's house through the chimney, maliciously intent on tormenting him. That was clear proof that Pinel was a warlock or, even worse, a true devil or *farfadet*, as Berbiguier liked to call the beings from hell. The *farfadets* and *farfadettes*—he also called the female imps *parafarquines*—were so insolent they once tumultuously followed him home from the Grand Penitentiary of Notre-

Dame with great scorn and derision. The First Restoration and les Cent-Jours scarcely intimidated the furies of the netherworld, who refused to let up their bedeviling of good Berbiguier.

All of these things were recounted in the three volumes of his autobiographical work *Les farfadets*, published in Paris in the year 1821. The edition is richly adorned with eight stupendous lithographs illustrating Berbiguier's vicissitudes. They are truly captivating. "The first lithograph," the author comments, "depicts me in the moment in which I decide to adopt the nickname of Fléau (Scourge) des Farfadets. The second portrays the room where Jeanneton Lavalette and la Mançot (witches, no doubt) reveal the Tarot before my eyes. In that moment I was under the influence of a malign planet; in the corners are two devils in the guise of a monkey and a bat. The third lithograph," continues Berbiguier, "shows an image of Rhotomago, followed by a bedraggled entourage of horned imps, coming to suggest I join their execrable fellowship. I reject them, indignant, as I stare fixedly at the Holy Cross of Our Lord Jesus Christ. The hell sent grow frightened at the sight of my bottle containing several thousand prisoners of their abominable army. In spite of it all, Rhotomago dares not raise his pitchfork against me. The fourth lithograph shows the scene with a firefighter as I was making my preparations to ensure a sunny, cloudless sky for the festival day of our good King (M. Berbiguier had burned sulfur to keep away the charming *farfadets* and the neighbors had called the fire department thinking there was a conflagration). In the fifth, I am seen preparing my potions with aromatic plants. The sixth depicts me continuing my preparation of the *antifarfadéen* remedy. I am seated beside my fireplace, at a table covered in pins, herbs, sulfur, salts, etc. There is also a bottle filled with captive demons. I observe my prisoners with a provocative gaze, but they are powerless to respond. Evil Pinel, armed with a pitchfork and accompanied by horrendous invisible beings, sought to terrorize me; but nothing can disrupt the tranquility of my senses. Étienne Prieur (a student of law), transformed into a pig, cannot resist the scent of my anti-infernal plants and he vomits up what he has perhaps ingested at the home of another of his victims. In the seventh lithograph appears a great concourse of demons, with Beelzebub and Rhotomago in the foreground. Among those in attendance are Monsieurs Pinel, Moreau, Chaix, and Étienne Prieur, the latter in pig guise as always and complaining of the pricking of my pins. Lastly, the eighth illustration is a portrait of hell with the infamous Belphegor and a he-goat. Among the crowd we find Jeanneton Lavalette, la Mançot, and la Vendaval. All the symbols around the image are magical symbols."

This edition of *Les farfadets* sold out quickly and was never reprinted. A few years ago, during the German occupation of Paris, General Ludwig von Wier found a complete copy of this extremely rare work and, ever since then, communicated with the *farfadets,* whom he subjected to a very harsh and scientific pro-German military reeducation. The Führer took great interest in this case and maintained lively discussions with Wier. Alas, the general disappeared in the most enigmatic of ways, leaving behind only his dentures.

THE MAN WHO LOVED KATIE KING

All morning amid the desert brambles, the blue jay, bird of azure flight, squawked and ran like a lunatic from one rock to the next, crouching in fear for no apparent reason, until Charlie was happily born into the world. The newborn opened his eyes to the light on a squalid ranch and bawled in the arms of his father, the brave Tom Sanders, who very carefully spat out his chewing tobacco and wiped his lips on the back of his hand before picking Charlie up. In the kitchen some steaming beans with pig's ear were boiling, and out in the corral, as usual, the hens scratched at the ground. Mrs. Sanders, from the bed, told her husband to put the baby down in his crib and go fetch a bucket of water from the pond.

Charlie's father died in 1820 in the Indian Wars and typhoid fever took his wife three years later. As such, Charlie became an orphan and, at six years old, he was entrusted to the care of an aunt who lived in Boston. She told him very proudly that his father had been a man of great physical resilience who once, at a fair, bought a bottle of hair-growing solution from a charlatan, thinking that it was eau-de-vie, and guzzled it down in one gulp. He'd spent several days on the border between life and death, but finally his strong constitution won out, and he survived. He was left, however, a bit soft in the head.

Charlie had a sad, ill-fated childhood. When he left school, he worked successively as an electrician, druggist, dental assistant, messenger, and office employee. In 1842 he made friends with a painter who'd won a gold medal for a *Dying Hercules*, named Samuel F. B. Morse, but who was now claiming to have invented the telegraph. Charlie was astonished. At once all messages traveled extremely quickly, and he watched them fly fantastically throughout the States of the Union. He was so applied in his learning of the telegraph that Morse named him his assistant, and he made much progress in the field of telecommunications. When Western Union and the American Telegraph Company exploited Morse's invention, Charlie's extraordinary knowledge got him named director of the latter, and he invented the telegraph pump and the wireless telegraph. It goes without saying that, before long, Charlie became a rich man.

One day, something truly strange happened to Charlie. He was in his office, immersed in a deep meditation on telegraphic subjects, when all of a sudden he saw a small corner table rise up from the ground, fly through the air at varying speeds, and land gracefully to one side of the door. Then he observed that, in the place where the table had always been, there was a pot with a gilded lily and a bed of ripe strawberries. Charlie rubbed his eyes, not believing what he was seeing. He tasted a strawberry and found it very good and very sweet smelling. That extraordinary occurrence made him ill, and he had to take to his bed for some time.

The events repeated when he returned to work. That altered the course of his life, since as soon as he closed the door to his office, he forgot all about the telegraph and anxiously waited for the show to unfold. He became melancholy. Things got more complicated, and disconcerting objects began to appear, like cavalry trumpets, embroidered pillows adorned with ribbons, bloody axes from the Sioux Wars, repulsive and broken sets of teeth. He wrote to the great spiritist Allan Kardec, asking if meddlesome spirits act out of personal animosity or random, unprovoked malice. His answer was, "Both. Sometimes they are enemies you've made, in this life or previous ones, seeking you out, and other times they have no motive whatsoever."

At the height of his befuddlement, just months later, Charlie was introduced, by Julia Ward Howe, feminist and writer of "The Battle Hymn of the Republic," to the chemist William Crookes, who'd recently arrived from London. Crookes, through the medium Florence Cook, managed to summon a well-known female spirit named Katie King. Miss King appeared swathed in transparent and perfumed white veils and was languid and beautiful. Charlie, upon seeing her, fell head over heels in love. He stopped worrying about the apparitions that haunted him and showed up at Crookes's sessions with his heart aflutter and a lovely bouquet of red roses, which he invariably and excitedly offered to Miss King. However, suddenly and with no prior warning, Miss King never reappeared again.

There were various versions of the affair. Around that time many fake mediums were unmasked, and it was said that, during their materializations, they would expel the ectoplasm they'd cleverly hidden in their mouths, carefully blowing it out into the darkness, and then at the end of the session they'd gather it up ignominiously into their most shameful recesses. This detail triggered a collapse in Charlie, and he had to be admitted to a public sanatorium.

American Telegraph paid for the finest doctors, who performed vigorous and revolutionary procedures. Nevertheless, Charlie continued to deteriorate. One April morning, the nurses walked in on Charlie reciting verbatim the entirety of the commentaries, or apparatus, by the glossator Irnerius on the text of the *Pandectae*. Seeing as he lacked the adequate legal training and had no knowledge of medieval Latin, that was a truly anomalous occurrence. It was only then, after much reflection, that the doctors declared him insane.

BRINDIS AT COVADONGA

In the States he didn't even like to tell people he was from and born in Mexico City, because it always seemed to bring up, to them, all sorts of images and assumptions that had nothing to do with his actual life and memory growing up in East Hollywood. His LA was Armenians, Turks, Lebanese, Filipinos and Thai and Cubanos, Blacks, Mexicanos, and Chicanos. Also aging and old white people who all seemed to wear funny hats. Lots of drunks and enough tecatos. On the streets too many prostitutes and homeless and wheelchair people. Nobody rich or close. Lots of fire trucks and ambulances, police cars and helicopters.

Samuel spoke Spanish like maybe a sixth-grader, English like a high-school dropout who got Ds and Fs. Which he got and was. But eventually he did all right. He got a great maintenance job in the nearby hospital where his mom was a housekeeper too, and he became the department's supervisor. He worked easy with everyone, married, bought a house, fathered two children, divorced, sold the house and let a judge split the gains and losses. He took the pension when it was a deal to retire, and now he wasn't young anymore. His children didn't live in LA. One was in the military, still in Afghanistan, the other, already three babies, was in Denver. They needed everything but him.

Samuel had gone to Mexico City over two weeks ago. He wasn't sure why he came but thought he might stay a while. It was more why not than because. The few people he called friends, though he barely ever spoke to them—he had time, they didn't—all said it was to go home. He resisted mocking that, as tiresome as it was. One longtime friend—he knew him from work alone—who was always very hippie-wise because he'd gone to college and so what he didn't finish, said that lots of animals go back to their "natal birthplace" to die. Samuel's first reaction was to cuss him and hang up for good. Let *him* die. Then as quickly came resignation and silence. The man had been this exact, deeper-than-thou jerk forever. That and a few more explained why Samuel became his boss, while he still carried screwdrivers around.

Samuel was on his way to see his sister-in-law, Flor, his older and only brother's smart Oaxacan wife. When he met her, she was still an india. Zapoteca.

She was not, like these brothers, mestizo. Roby went crazy for her, everything about her, and everything she believed in—so it seemed to Samuel. Roby was born Roberto. Once their mother moved them all to the States, the schools made him Robert. To everybody else, Robbie. He went back to *la capital* often—unlike Samuel, he missed it, and traveled back whenever he could, staying with grandparents and friends he made growing up. He was good at art, talented, and then he met Flor. There he became Roby—not pronounced like a robber but a rower—while she preferred to be called an indigena. By his later twenties, he never came back to the States—except for trips to New York—even to see his mom (their dad had abandoned them early along). She went to see them more often when Roby and Flor had babies, though she never accepted the invitation to live with them. Roby's art sold in Europe and China, and they seemed to be living well. Art was everywhere in their home, canvases leaning, hanging, stacked, piled sideways, and stored in every otherwise unoccupied space. Samuel couldn't go to visit much if at all because of his work—which didn't pay enough for trips either—and he didn't really want to because he always felt out of his element. Like Roby and Flor were from a faraway, better, and more exotic land than where he was raised. His brother was both more native and worldly, one whose life was as mysterious to him as it was obvious—as bright as yellow red and blue oil paint. And then, years ago already, suddenly, he died.

———

Samuel never thought about taxis in the States—like he ever had a reason to— but here this luxury transportation to him was two or three dollars. He even learned to Uber.

"I love your wheels," he told the driver. It was a glossy black Toyota, not new, but kept in excellent condition.

The driver eyed him through the mirror. "I am sorry, but I don understand," he said in English.

"I'm sorry," Samuel said in Spanish. "I forgot where I was. All this green here. Nothing like where I live."

The driver still saw him from his rearview. "Where are you from?"

"The States. Where else?"

"Could be many countries," the driver said. "I see people from all over the world."

Samuel nodded. "It's so beautiful," he said. Better after enough days, he still had to think of words and sentences before he spoke. "Like a garden... in the... I don't remember the word... where Tarzan lived... green, everywhere green green, big green plants."

"*Selva*," the driver suggested.

"Yes, that's it. I can't remember so many words. Or I never knew them. The simplest ones, you know?"

The driver spoke at him through the rearview. "But you know Spanish enough."

"I was born here."

"In Mexico?"

"Yes, right here, in Mexico City." He wanted to tell him how he knew that was hard to believe, but that was too complicated. "It's so beautiful," he said again instead. "My sister-in-law told me that... that that was what the conquistadors said when they first saw it here." Samuel had gone with Flor and one of her daughters, his niece, to the Zócalo a week before for the five-hundred-year anniversary of the defeat of the Aztecs and destruction of Tenochitlan by the Spanish.

The driver listened, eyes driving, GPS guiding.

"So this is how you make a living?" Samuel asked. "With Uber? It's good? Enough?"

The driver turned his eyes into the mirror. "I've only done this for a few months now. It's not so bad. I'm sixty-seven. I couldn't find any other job. It's been very hard."

"Because you're old, or because of the pandemic?"

"The two," the driver said.

"But you have... *social security?* For your old age?"

"¿Cómo?"

"A pension," said Samuel.

The driver shook his head calmly and drove.

"Not from the government. Not from your job?"

"I worked many years, all my life," the driver said easily. "In radio and television. I loved my job. But it was always as a contractor. *Freelance*, in English.

And I saved nothing. The work was slowing for me and stopped over a year ago. All work. A friend told me about doing this Uber."

"Radio and television. Wow. That's good work. You have to know… things. Smart things." He thought about how little this trip was costing. "And now Uber."

The driver told Samuel names of the TV and radio programs he'd worked for. Samuel knew none, but they were all clearly well-known in the city and maybe country—the driver's pride glowed in the mirror, even though his voice stayed even, calm. Another person might have turned and looked right at Samuel when he mentioned one name, a star or famous host he'd worked for the longest.

Samuel responded spontaneously. "How great is that?" he said, no idea of who or what.

"A long time," the driver told him. "I never thought…"

"I'm lucky," Samuel said, "because I didn't either."

———

Samuel and Flor were going to visit a realtor about a foreclosed house in San Ángel. He didn't know anything about these matters, but Flor thought that his presence might add somehow. She said she loved her home, their family home for so many decades, but maybe it would be best if she sold it and left. Things were bad for everyone. But if she could get that house, that property, for that price they were quoting… though she didn't want to move. It just seemed smarter if she did. Samuel didn't think to ask her if she was in trouble somehow. His brother was always rich to him.

As Samuel was waiting to pass through the wrought iron gate after he'd buzzed her, a man, dressed well, came out the door leaving. Flor's dog was going wild deciding which man was more important. As Samuel walked inside, Flor's two cats both came to him like dogs wanting to smell.

"I thought he would take two or even three more paintings to sell," she said.

"And instead he wanted… directions, or maybe a date?"

She didn't go along. "They're not selling."

"Roby's paintings?"

"It's a bad day," she said.

He waited a bit for her. Then, "But you still want to go?"

"Yes, we will go."

He petted a cat and the dog at the same time. It was unnaturally quiet, not usual.

She offered him coffee and warmed some for them both and sat at the table across from him.

"Don Emiliano died today," she finally said.

He couldn't register what she was telling him.

"He drove us. Everywhere, all the time. That man."

"The taxi driver? The one you always… every time I've ever been here. A couple of days ago."

"He was more part of our family. He even knew my mother."

"I even remember him from all the years back," Samuel said again.

Flor didn't seem to have much more to add.

"When?" asked Samuel.

"This morning. His son called me an hour ago."

They sipped the coffee.

She said, "Do you know that today is the anniversary of Roby's death?"

Samuel didn't say no but didn't have to.

"He died here on this day. He didn't want to go to the hospital to die. He wanted it to be here, with us."

Samuel had come for the funeral, but there was much he didn't know. "Well, I don't think we should go today. It is a bad day, like you told me."

"I can go," Flor said. "We have the appointment."

"I don't think we should. We shouldn't go. Not today."

She agreed. She called to postpone.

"I can leave, too," Samuel said. "Maybe you have other things, or you want to be alone, or…"

"No no, stay. You can stay."

"We can have cena as we planned. Something here, or maybe good to go out."

"Whatever you say," he said. "What's best for you."

"I know where we want to go," said Flor after a few moments.

———

A random taxi drove them at the beginning of the evening's rain. It was a light drizzle, almost a mist, and it made all seem shaded lush, a tropical green. The restaurant was the Covadonga. Samuel remembered it going with both Roby and Flor and also with Roby alone, though he was never alone, especially here. Everybody knew him, and he knew everybody. The entrance canopy that reached the street, with its coat of arms and logo and even a doorman, was more New York than Mexico. It saved them from getting wet. Up a few stairs they entered a huge hall, to a Mexican cantina bigger than one in any American western movie. So many tables, for whatever the party size—tablecloths and napkins pressed and folded, dinnerware sparkling—spread around generously, TVs on the wing-side walls, a long wooden bar at the wall facing. But the Covadonga's cantina style wasn't of a dusty charro era of horses and broad sombreros, haciendas and Pancho Villa. It was from the 40s and 50s, when cars were heavy and slow, waiters dressed like French officers, the Spanish food was for the higher class.

"When I come here I think of happy times," Flor told Samuel.

"It's pretty great," he said. "Even I remember one really fun night drinking too much here."

"Loud and noisy, busy," she said. "Singing and laughing. Gritos. Happiness."

A waiter came and she greeted him by his first name. He called her doña Flor. They both talked about it being too long. She ordered a gin and tonic. Samuel ordered a beer, but the label's *especial* just to be a little more classy than he was.

"What a good idea," he told her.

The drinks arrived with a formal grace.

"*Un brindis,*" Flor pronounced. She raised her glass. "To don Emiliano. My whole family loved him. I loved him, and I will miss him."

They clinked and sipped.

"To Roby," Samuel said, his beer glass forward, "and to your love of him." Again they clinked and sipped.

"To México," she said before he relaxed, "and for the five hundred years before, too." That was for them to smile.

Some friends from a table across the restaurant approached her, and then she went to their table for a while to speak to an elderly man and came back.

"He is at least a hundred years old, even more. He always seemed as old as México. Of course he too knew Emiliano. So small our world. His older sister was who first took him in. Don Emiliano was eleven and he wore mismatched shoes and he wanted a job, any job whatever. He never wanted to go back to what was supposed to be his home. He would never drink. And always he worked more than anyone to raise his family."

They didn't wait long for their food. She got a bean stew from Asturias, and he got a paella from Valencia.

"Did you know that the Spaniards tortured Cuauhtémoc after they captured him? They said he was hiding gold, maybe even in his body. And here we are, choosing their food."

"But didn't you tell me that if the Aztecs…"

"*Los mexicas…*"

"…had it their way, we'd be eating conquistador thighs?" Samuel said. "I barely eat fish, and yeah I eat chickens and cows, but I'm not eating no Spaniard even if I want him worse than dead."

"Might be tasty. Especially in Oaxacan mole. *Con chocolate.*"

Samuel kept laughing. Hers went shorter.

"Ours was a culture of much natural beauty," she said. "But we fought too much among ourselves, hating each other. Cortés should have never gotten close. No one can ever know what we could have been, what we could have taught and learned from one another."

Samuel tried to keep it light. "You wish you were still barefoot, making tortillas?"

"Well, I love *las mujeres* making *las tortillas*," Flor told him. "I love tortillas. I love our corn. I love our earth and our rain and our sun. I am proud of us. We are the people of *esta tierra*. It isn't always easy, but así es."

She waited for him but Samuel wasn't used to this talk. When the bill came, he said, "Let me buy tonight." They usually divided all evenly. "Please, it's on me."

———

Because it had to be a day for hard rain, it was. They'd left before the downpour, but inside Samuel's rental, rain was puddling through the windows or walls to the floor. He had only one towel—besides the one he selfishly kept for showering—but he didn't have three more, what it would take, if it didn't last too much longer. He kept his shoes on. Choosing this place was his kind of mistake—it was cheaper than that one, or that, and what great difference except the price? This was him since the beginning, who he was.

In fact the rented departamento was like his earliest memories of being in México. The tiny kitchen, barely big enough for a stove and a refrigerator it wasn't designed for. The bathroom that smelled of leaky toilet. The window views of the tattered interior ductwork of the old building, or, its exterior side of the glass probably not washed since its installation, a handsome plot of garbage dump land. Faint lighting, like the mental light of his memory, like the reality of the dim bulbs hanging on their electrical wires from the ceiling holes. He didn't remember furniture, and this place, but for a sofa chair covered by a Mexican blanket, had none. What he remembered from his earliest childhood was how every inside space for play had its danger. That was part of whatever game imagined. He had no toys that he could remember. What he had was Robbie. He was the best toy. He was safety and light wherever there was darkness.

He turned a large-screen TV on. It was part of the sell of this place, and it was accurate. Connection fuzz and interruptions aside, he could watch a Dodger game on the deportes channel. The color on the TV, the only light, was a mural on the drab wall. He was in México. He got in the bed and paid attention to the rain after many booms of thunder and sharp strikes of lightning. It was not an LA rainstorm until it calmed.

The trembling after that calm began slowly, but the seconds were enough for Samuel to be aware and pull on pants and slip on socks and shoes and stand. The TV blanked and then darkness. His left hand went to the wall as a guide and balance. The plaster had become plastic, molten, wavy. He grabbed up his phone. He felt it was his own anxiety making the room seem to roll up and down. He heard voices in the building's hallway and feet pounding down the stairs. The room began rocking and even in the darkness a white dust seemed to be a spray of light and he heard a large chunk of something thudding on one side of his door or the other. He decided to stand in the doorjamb he was near, his hands gripping, arms pressing either side. His eyes, watching everywhere they could, his brain preparing for a drop under him or a sudden falling from above. But it stopped. The seconds, maybe forty-five, maybe sixty, seemed long and he waited more seconds. Electricity came back and he moved more. He opened his door. The chunk, window-sized, was from an upper corner, his door side. The door of the departamento across was open and he walked there and looked inside and said hello hello and no one. Outside people milled about. He went back up.

The television was on again and he changed it to news. They were gathering information on the magnitude and damage. The phone rang.

"You're fine?" Flor asked him.

"I'm shaky," he said. "I don't know what to do. I've always been scared... though never the little ones I've felt in LA."

"Nothing to do," she said.

"Where are you?" he asked.

"At a wake for don Emiliano."

"Really?... Nothing happened there?"

"It shook all, all of us. For a moment. But... I am glad I was here. I am still."

"You're not worried about your home?"

"Not enough, no. I'm sure it will be fine."

"Okay then," he said.

"Aren't you glad to be back where you're from?" she teased him.

Samuel laughed as she wanted him to.

"Thank you," he told her. "I should have come back sooner."

"You're here now," she joked. "Like you never left."

GHOSTS

I.   ## XEROX CHARTS

In the summer of 1982, my father took the inheritance left by his father and bought $50,000 dollars of Xerox stock. He had been researching the advance of the computer and felt Xerox would be an important part of it. He had a few other stocks, small things that came up during his research, but the bulk of the stake was in Xerox. He held it for years, and then, despite nearly no trading experience, sold at its peak in 1999, right before the dot-com bubble burst. He had bought at just over twelve dollars a share and sold at nearly $150 a share, giving him half a million dollars. The government took their cut, but what they didn't take he used to purchase a home on the Cape.

Why did you buy and *why did you sell* can be two of the most interesting questions that you can ask someone with this story. They're not simple questions, and it's not really about money. When someone holds for years it becomes something they've lived inside. You can feel the stock's movements, and can feel when it's losing strength. At first everyone says it's your psyche, that's all, that it's going to keep climbing, but you can feel it, you can feel the floor going ahead of time. You just don't completely admit it, so it's hard to tell. But, also, pressure mounts, there's now something you can lose that you didn't have before, so you get the jitters, and maybe that's what you're seeing instead, ghosts trying to take the money.

Why Xerox, one asks. I know, he says, Why not Apple. Why not Apple. What's the difference, he used to say, except a view of the sea. His home was nestled in the scrub of the Cape. Apple would have got him on a ledge overlooking the sea, but when he said that, he had been living in that home so long he would have never wanted anything else. His name for the house was the Xerox Fortune. And here is the Xerox Fortune he might say when welcoming someone in, even if they didn't know the story, so they might wonder at his tie to the founding family or what the house might have had to do with photocopiers. It's not the Apple fortune, but it'll do for now. I wondered back then what would happen to the Xerox Fortune after he died, if, one day in my will, I would be passing the home down to my son in the way that ghosts once created don't disappear. This comment sounds dramatic, and I don't mean that, that the loss of my dad's fortune (for he didn't pass the house to me in his will and instead donated it to the Modern House Trust. I've since seen the house twice on tour, and for a time you could rent it overnight, though I hadn't done that. He also donated money for its upkeep. He left me what money remained, which wasn't a large amount but was not inconsequential to my life), I don't mean that the loss haunted me and my son. I just mean ghosts in the sense that once fear or love creates another presence, it follows along always. My dad's moment of gripping that stock, of researching into the night, trying to understand if that shaking he felt—which would result in the loss of nearly the worth of the Xerox stock— if that movement was simply his fear, or if he could trust his understanding of the tremor and that it meant to get out.

It feels, looking back at bubbles, that it's one movement. Everything was rocketing in price, and then it collapsed. But when I think about my father holding Xerox, it wouldn't have been as simple as he had it, then sold, and then it collapsed. It would have been several movements and each would have its own decision. I must have asked him at some point how he had handled those months, but I'm not sure he had a clear answer or, if he did, then I don't recall it. The thing is, if it had been Amazon you held at that time, then buying back in, even if you did it too early, that would have been the right thing. But that hadn't been the case with Xerox. He had played it perfectly.

During the time I was researching this, I was still at home. Thom was in Boston. So nothing had changed, but around us there were changes, and you felt them in your own way. To fall asleep I read about the dot-com bubble. I would watch the markets in the morning and then would drive to the harbor of a neighboring town simply to be at another harbor.

There were dozens of midcentury homes sprinkled throughout the lower Cape, built in the woods, near ponds, some designed by locals and some by Bauhaus members like Marcel Breuer. Most were rustic wood homes with large windows, but my father's was a brutalist concrete structure. In pictures it's rather ugly, for the magic of the work is in its proportions, as if someone with a sense of humor had shrunk a very serious home and that was the house my father selected, though he didn't, for the most part, have a sense of humor. He must have preferred the style and failed to notice the joke of the dimensions. It also didn't have many windows. Perhaps because of the concrete used, only the top was well lit—for though small, it climbed to three floors, with the telescope room inset on all sides with high windows and a pitched glass roof. When we talked, we mostly sat in that top room. He had thin white skin and blue eyes and all the light created a sort of transparency in him.

He'd have me carry one of the metal trays up from the kitchen with a teapot and cups. Little saucers of something or another, figs, Italian cookies. It was an open galley kitchen that had no cabinets, only shelves and hooks, so my father just kept what was necessary and each item was out as if waiting for its immediate use. The dish cloth on a hook next to the sink, an aluminum strainer, four Russel Wright mugs. He had been an environmentalist who wrote early about the coming of the computer, the dangers of climate change, the land struggles of the Native Americans, but in all the writing he was encyclopedic, dry, the legalities of each case captured in detail and only sometimes did the people come through, as if he could see them, but only from time to time. It was a wonder, then, how much my father loved beauty. His bedroom was spare except for a bed with a wool Native American blanket in earth tones and valuable framed line drawings.

Outside, surrounding a patio with an iron table set, he grew many kinds of sage. His office looked over this garden and I remember once, while making dinner, going to pick sage and seeing him at his desk through the glass door and noticing that his back was turned away from the garden. Who turns away from the garden, I wondered. I was panfrying fish and serving it with new potatoes. It wasn't long after my divorce. I was staying for a week in his extra bedroom. He had always liked my husband, liked that he was a mathematician and liked staying up late talking to him. It was perhaps easier for him then when I was there alone. He used to buy several nice bottles of French wines when we visited having learned this was what my ex-husband preferred. This time I had tried to improve our chances by having him invite a few friends to dinner. One night he had over a man who caned chairs. Another night he had the conservationist over. I had said I would make dinner but then didn't buy enough fish. There were several loaves of bread from the French bakery and good butter. The man then brought an olive loaf. We had a tremendous amount of bread. They had a conversation about my father's pottery that I hadn't understood. My father had been carefully purchasing a vintage collection piece by piece. Everything inside the home was from the appropriate time period. The blinds, the carpets, the pen set on his desk. He said something about the pottery as if here were giving it to the man. Why would he be gifting the dishes we were eating off of? The conservationist was a sensitive man in his late forties in a tweed cap. I didn't find him handsome but was otherwise drawn to him because he had a certain kind of sadness. It was a soft sort of feeling—it wouldn't overwhelm and instead would probably make him a good listener. He didn't pursue the comment my father made about the pottery. He asked me about my life in New York. I'm going through a rather difficult divorce at the moment, I said.

Oh yes, he said, allowing that he'd also had one.

A mathematician, my father said, a bright man.

Oh yes, the man repeated.

I'm so sorry about the fish, I said.

It's nothing. Never mind about the fish, my father said. He refilled our glasses. It was a good bottle of wine.

After the man left, we washed the dishes, my father at the sink and me standing next to him drying. He had taken off his dress shirt and wore an undershirt. Why not another shot at it, Janey, my father said. This was the hundredth shot, I said. Oh, he said. Oh, taking a sponge to the mixing bowl. It's not like you think it might be, he said, where you'll have so many other chances, but if you've given it time, and it hasn't helped, sometimes that's all that can be done.

All the beautiful Russel Wright pottery laid on a dishtowel. I find I want to talk about visiting the Russel Wright house along the Hudson River, a trip I made with a friend when I was pregnant, so far along that I was close to not being able to travel. We ate at a café that made their own hard cider, and I drank a sip from my friend's glass, and we stopped after at the Rockefeller Church where I rested in the pew and looked at the Chagall windows. I find I want to talk about the delicateness of the Russell Wright home. That quality reminded me of Fallingwater, something that you aren't able to tell from pictures. I've toured, whenever I travel, many of these kinds of homes, and prefer the smaller ones, the ones where you can tell how someone has lived. I find it easier, of course, to go to those places than to stay in the kitchen with my father, recalling him in that unguarded moment, in his undershirt, bending over the sink, the spot beneath his nape showing wayward hairs. I also don't remember it well. It wasn't a dramatic scene when I learned I wasn't getting the house. I understood. It probably wasn't that night. Though I remember parts of that night well. The divorce, the sudden and surprising failure of my nervous system, the difficulties I had in sleeping leading me to get up and make snacks that I ate off of paper towels. The smell of the conservationist when he took off his coat, like the old nutmeg we use once a year in cookies.

II.   **COMPOSITION DOLLS**

My father never told the story of his breakdown or the recovery. He never said why. He always rushed to the part of the story that interested him, which was all the abandoned farmhouses in New Hampshire. He had driven there from his family's home in Connecticut and broke into one to sleep, perhaps feeling he might end his life there, though that thought was let go of early, for much in the landscape and old buildings ended up interesting him. One thought he had trouble letting go of was that there was a second farmhouse just the same as the one he was in, and he was also in that one. His was a bare, white farmhouse that glowed when the afternoon light hit. That was when he felt there was another farmhouse, also a bare thing in a field, alight. He would drive in the morning to a gas station for coffee and then look for the other farmhouse. He knew it was there. He just had to drive around long enough. The problem, though, the problem that he couldn't work out was what finding it would mean, because he didn't think that inside would be another him, or inside would be a portal to another place. He hadn't entirely detached from reality. He knew that when he found the second farmhouse, he would enter in the same way he had entered the other and that he would stand in the lit windows and feel the same desire, maybe a little stronger, and eventually the light would go down, and that would be what he would find and nothing else.

Did you find the farmhouse? I asked.

What? he said, confused by the question, though he had just detailed the days of looking. No, no, he said, as if I had missed the point of the story. No, the weather changed, there was a deep freeze, and I went back.

People do this, he knew as well as I did, find great loves, have epiphanies, and then if you ask them what came of it, there's never another part of the story, except that something else happens, usually quite apart from that.

My father was in my life because he had run into my pregnant mother at the Riverbend. He had returned to the Cape months after the night he met her at the bar , and he drank sometimes there. Though she was quite pregnant, he said nothing about it, even offering to buy her a drink. It's soda water, she said, pointing to her glass, so he ordered her that then sat there. He explained that he would be returning to the Cape frequently then asked if they could stay in touch. I'd like to help in any way, my father said. Already then, in that moment, began the seed of wanting me. What do we think children offer us? Even growing inside of us, even when we become, for a short time, a doubled self, even then we don't have access to them. When I lay in bed, pregnant, tired from my shift, holding my stomach so I could feel his body, his elbow perhaps, through my skin, watching whatever the antenna of my old TV picked up—the Kentucky Derby that year had a horse going for the Triple Crown, but I fell asleep and woke hours later to muted golf commentary—even then my son was separate from me.

My father visited her from time to time while she was pregnant. He helped her bring a carload of stuff up when she moved. It seemed she asked everyone she knew to take over a box. Well, she was beautiful, even pregnant. Finally, as if this were the thing they had been talking about, and it had at last been decided, she said, I don't think it's yours. When he didn't answer, she said, I thought you would want to know, that it was what you'd been wondering. There was something, someone else, earlier. It's not, he said. It probably was, but the idea of it would have seemed reductive to him.

When I was a little girl, my father developed an interest in antique dolls and he would take me to flea markets and we'd bring them back to the furnished apartment he rented down Cape.

He found a doll with eyes that were crystallized, crazy looking. She'll look fine with a little work, the woman at the table said. It's just the rust behind them, you would just use a drop of oil. I might like them this way, my father said. Or sometimes people replace them, the woman said, but that's more work. My father bought the doll and went home and sat at the kitchen table, detaching the doll at the neck. I sat next to him eating a bag of dried nectarines. He studied the doll, looking inside the body and at last said, I see. He picked up the head and heated it with a blow-dryer he had found under the sink and removed the eyes. The doll sat there for several days with empty eye sockets. He would be going back to Boston after he dropped me off at home. He said he would look for new eyes there. What color do you think? he said.

Blue, I said.

Why blue? I shrugged. The ocean, is that it? Do you want to walk out to the water before dinner? I shrugged again. I can't see you shrugging while I'm working.

We drove to Truro and parked on the side of Route 6 then walked the mile of dunes to the ocean. Later in life I would travel to the south of France and stay with a friend in a family home in a small village. Sometimes we drove to neighboring villages to buy wine or cheese or sausages, but other times we stayed home and drank pastis in the village square. I would take long walks in the afternoon while he worked. Something had happened that made me unhappy, some bit of heartbreak, and I was too restless to sit and read, and he had shown me a few trails, one that ended at a plum tree. I had thought before the trip that the countryside would be gentle and soothing, but in fact it wasn't that way, it was arid, desolate, quite beautiful but not in a calming way, instead in a way that cast your loneliness back at you. The landscape of the Cape was quite different but also had that quality. The endless stretches of the dunes down Cape played with scale, it made you feel, not necessarily your loneliness, though perhaps you felt that, too, but more your smallness. Everyone's smallness, so it created a tableau, or an abstraction of your family—your father as a slight figure climbing a hill of sand in a khaki cap. When we got to the shoreline we swam for a little then walked back.

She was a sleeping doll, so her eyes were attached to a weighted metal bar called a rocker inside her head. He found another set and then another. None of them fit the doll, but that, after a time, wasn't the point. He had become a collector of antique-glass doll eyes. I showed them to Thom one night. Well, not the collection, long lost, but pages of them on eBay, one pair with lashes of human hair, another with a more elegant metal contraption, another with the eyes still set in damaged plaster. The eyes looked startled to be out of the heads, as one would imagine human eyes would look, though I wouldn't have thought it of doll eyes, where once inset they look placid, harmless. Thom asked if I was going to order any, and I said that I didn't think so, though that wasn't the truth. On Craigslist, I had found a composition doll with sleeping eyes in Manchester. She was photographed naked but listed as coming in the dress that she had been found in. I had liked those last words—*that she had been found in*—and I wrote to see if I could buy her.

I drove out to Manchester, telling Thom I was working at the library so that he would pick Lawrence up from school. The woman met me in her driveway with a box. She looked at me as if trying to understand something then said it was her mother's and she was born in 1948, so she must be from the fifties. I gave her the ten dollars.

At home, I stuck the box under our bed and forgot about her until Thom left for New York for a few shows. I had by then learned about cleaning the doll, that I shouldn't wash and shampoo her as I had intended, as that would deteriorate the body, and so I took off her dress and brushed her with a clean toothbrush. And then I brought her to the kitchen table, and I pulled at her head. I had read that eyes could sometimes be accessed under the skull as well, so I tugged at her wig. I didn't want to damage her, though, so after a time I put her back in the box and opened a beer and waited for the show to be done and for Thom to call.

I liked the doll and felt there was a human quality to her—as that Craigslist woman must have felt as well, calling the doll *her* and not *it*—but I found it was the eyes I wanted or felt I needed. I had taught Hoffman's story "The Sandman" and Freud's "The Uncanny" for years without being able to pin down what was uncanny about dolls. I felt it had something to do with the eyes and that they were in pairs and not single. The Sandman is a mythical creature that comes at night and throws sand in children's faces and takes their eyes. The main character of Hoffman's story believes that it's the Sandman who has killed his father. Later in the story, the Sandman makes an automaton, a mechanical doll, and the main character falls in love with it. Any life she possesses seems to be in her eyes, though those ultimately fall out. Eyes are mentioned often in the story—they get made, or go missing, or show love—as if, if a human were able to make eyes, then they would be able to make life. Here, eyes aren't the window to the soul, eyes are the soul; if one made eyes, then the soul, too, would be made.

And when Freud talks about the Hoffman story in his essay "The Uncanny," he calls the damage or loss of eyes our most primal childhood fear but then ruins the thought by saying it stands in for our fear of castration. Maybe it's more useful to talk about our desire for eyes, why the myth of the Sandman is driven by a desire for eyes and for taking out eyes, and why, when my father got his doll, that was what he did, and why, when faced with my doll at the kitchen table, that was what I wanted.

Freud would call the feeling the uncanny, a feeling of the workings of another world on an object of this one, that thing being endowed by tracings of primitive thought or repression of our childhoods. He said that often children, when playing with dolls, don't differentiate whether they are living or not, and so to them, the lifelikeness of dolls isn't uncanny.

I collected doll eyes with rollers—Thom brought me a pair he had found while traveling, and I ordered several pairs—and kept them in a cabinet in the bedroom. One night he watched at the table as I took off a doll's wig and reached in for the eyes. At my concern he said, She's not alive. It's beautiful how it works, I said, looking into the head while I sat her up and then lay her down, watching the lids fall down. We watched it several times, then I put the wig back on and put her away. Thom was careful with me during this time. He understood, I thought, the doll more than I did. But it turned out that he felt he might love someone else and was treating me gently as a result.

He told me everything a few days later: It was a woman in a band that he had played with in Saint Louis and had known, indirectly, for years. What do we know of love, of course, "The Sandman" asks, as the character falls in love with a doll, a delusion perhaps caused by a new pair of glasses. Thom moved out of the house. I made tea. I sat at the table. Sometimes we talked on the phone. He went to visit her and that confused him and her. I thought about the way he said *her*, like the doll had been referred to in the ad. That it signified life. And she did develop a life inside me that grew as he talked about her. Once, during this time, he said, Do you ever imagine how difficult you can be? How you can sound? I always thought it was precision, that I was very precise. It didn't feel like coldness. For instance, I wanted to know what the woman looked like and so googled her band, and she was pretty with long black hair and a cute plaid skirt, and it hurt, but the details also felt significant, more significant than what I might feel or not feel.

One day I went to see Thom in Boston. He was subletting a loft space with factory-size windows and a counter with a sink and hot plate and microwave. He made a french press and we sat on stools at the counter. He talked about music, about his new album, and asked what I had been doing, and I explained that I had been trying with our friend Derek to make glass.

It had occurred to me that the heart of the Sandman story might lay in the process of making eyes, in how difficult they were to make. If those characters were attempting to create life, then the extraordinary heat needed to create glass would be the largest obstacle. I always thought it was a story about childhood loneliness, Thom said before asking if I was sleeping with Derek.

What do you think?

That you are?

I'm not, I said. It was entirely an interest in glass. We had talked about it already on the phone, but Thom had forgotten. I had told him that I'd asked Derek to make doll's eyes and Thom said that Derek wouldn't be able to make glass eyes, and then I said that Derek made stained glass, and Thom had said that doesn't mean you make the glass. You just make stained glass by melting glass? I said, frustrated.

Glass takes over 2,000 degrees to make, but Derek had a friend with a kiln, so I ordered the sand and was waiting for it to come in. That was how the father died in the story—not by the Sandman or any magical properties—but simply by a blast from the furnace.

Thom was going to the South End to buy an instrument and wanted me to come. There was a large estate-sale store there. We could walk around and get a sandwich after. We were still in his apartment and had switched from coffee to bottles of Corona. I don't think so, I said.

You know, he said, that people make mistakes, sometimes very large ones.

I make mistakes all the time.

That we are imperfect creatures. You know that, right?

We are perfect creatures, I said. This was not evidently true at the time, but if you've had a child and watched them sleep, it becomes true. When my son was born, I was surprised when the nurses used this word, and not as a compliment, but more to warn about the defects that babies can have. He's perfect, one said, in a voice implying that I should be thankful. But that's not quite it… thankful. I'm having trouble putting my finger on the word. Not thankful. And she did mean it as a compliment, a word said for my benefit, a new mother all alone. It just didn't ring that way in my ear. It felt cruel. Why was mine better than another's? A second nurse, finding a small flaw—a slight tongue-tie—said, Well, you can't have perfection, you know, as if that was, after all, what I was demanding. Though maybe I had been hoping for that unknowingly. Thinking of this I looked in Hoffman's story to see what they call the automaton they created, thinking perhaps they, too, called it perfect, but it wasn't there. Nothing about perfection, just a lot about laboring over what they produced.

It's beautiful, I told Thom, finally, the way the light comes in here. I don't blame you in a way.

In a way?

In all ways, in all ways I don't blame you. I just don't know if I can do this.

It occurred to me sometime later—after Derek and I failed to produce enough heat in the kiln, and after I ordered sets of eyes from eBay, one set and then another, and after I stripped the eyes from my doll—to realize that I had once made eyes, and not glass eyes, but actual eyes. I don't know why it hadn't occurred to me before, or to Hoffman even, that half of humanity is capable of making eyes, and the ones I made were muted gray blue, so muted they appeared brown.

NIGHT SKY WITH BLUE SILO AND A BONFIRE

IDRA NOVEY

We chopped down the weeds that hurt, the burdock
with its burrs that dug into the skin. We cut the nettles,
all the stinging weeds that stuck to us and to the sheep,
that lodged in the paws of the dogs, pricked us
through our shoes and jeans, wounded our hands
when we moved through the field, wanting to feel
something wild within ourselves. No matter where
on the stem my son gripped the nettles, no matter what
chopping tool he brought from the barn, the weeds
got hold of him anyhow. J's whole back turned
into a map of burrs, his same back struck last year
by a car, the back he bent now to feed the fire, bent
with his long responsibility for his mother, and his despair
at how fast she was going blind. We all bent, attempted
to get the burdock out of each other's hair as our heap
blazed high enough to heat our faces
when we drew close enough—and we drew that close
over and over, poking the flames with our sticks,
with our half-built houses and our mounting debts,
with our misspoken words and cancer scares, with our dread
for the whole heating earth. We leaned into the weedfire
with all the wavering love we could endure receiving
from each other. With three flashlights between us, we slashed
and yanked at more in the dark, knowing the burdock
would seed and grow right back—release new burrs
into the wooly sides of the sheep, and whoever of us
was not ill or gone, still getting along and not too caught up
chopping at other fields, would be lucky to bend here again,
cut down a day's worth of spiky burrs just to ignite them,
watch their hot shapes reflect on the blue metal of the silo.
To behold this fire of stinging weeds even once together
felt extraordinary, to see the smoke of what stung
rising right in front of us, light against the night sky.

SOMETHING ROUGHSPUN

JOANNA KLINK

between the blue spread of
farms and that freezing
city, driving without sleep
to see you, even then unable
to understand, mile markers
ticking past my eyes in
dim streams—That is all
you thought you could do,
you'd said, and it doesn't
hurt that you seemed closer
for those few minutes, the rain
coming loose in fine mirrors,
and exactly how are you shut
away from me now, having
left ourselves behind, like children
helpless and constantly
sorting, despite the private
motions of my voice, failing
the curve we began through
a life, my dark extinguished
eyes letting highways blaze
through them, so that
who you are now is nothing I
know but you were once all my
hopes, without any reliable
plot how should we have
guessed when restlessness sheered
past our bodies, even now
unnatural to pull myself
away—though it has been
years since you wrote my name
or stomped through the woods

or argued against the zeros
piling up in my throat—
because I was young and
could not understand
how hard it is to reach
anyone—or saw that this
might be what we share of
the future—an apartment I reached
late in the night, empty-handed,
convinced, in love
with every kind of closeness
you held out to me.

VIRIDARIUM

JOANNA KLINK

While I waited on the steps, wrapping
my arms around my knees,
I must have understood the change
that was coming, the flowers
in the yard rising intensely into
air. I look out now and see leaves,
already particular and shattered,
growing on the oak. It is not
only land that seems to lean up
toward me, but last night's thick rains
soaked below it and, outside this city,
the clay beneath fields.
Whatever I hoped for had to be
tempered. Ordinary. Flames
bending through rainfall.
And the clocks I discounted,
and the hardships—I held on,
like a bird filling with the sky
through which it moves. In this
late hour, falling from my own life,
you are the far tundra below,
astral heat against an empty
riverbed. There is a way to you
you said, staring at me across the table—
a willow's release of branches
in wind, a gateway opened
sparingly. We see the delicate
daily crushing of small things,
insects beneath matted
grasses. I must have known,
as a child, to leave my body
in order to be. I am trying

to let you arrive, to let the days
be armored and dark—obsidian,
glinting, or muscle shadowing
bone, seawater pushing inland,
the brush of night rains.
Our bodies altogether rinsed
of the light of being seen.

DUET

ATSURO RILEY

But that that brace of brothers pleached a song

Had we voice *!*

a voice

a braid-reed voice

our good throats restored

(our lockstitch chord)

We would croodle-keen

(could breathe)

our lodged our

locked unsaids—

Duet our not-thought knowns—

———

That this fear-axe weighs caustic on the walls of the mind.

That it gibbet-looms over us gleam-breathing pendulating all the time fixing to fall.

That a body gets (a soul gets) fostered same by beauty sure by fear.

That sure as fangs a threat-pestered sheeny cottonmouth gon' gape.

That this whip-shape underfoot in pinestraw: more a diamondback turned flinchy.

That the (leaf-crinching) coldcoiled copperheads will spring.

That once upon a switchblade spring a man a crudded truck coerced us off.

That the annals they will show how young and green.

That a snappin' turtle's jawbeak (puncts you like a bear-trap) stays sunk in meat till lightning.

That some are bent to hunt to use a thing or eat or crush it since they can.

That we ourselves would kick-dent and axe-batter any innocent flank of galvanize for noise.

That anyhow trust the skinny scenthounds to backtrack more or less their track to home exactly.

That our mother salt-saves food for the end of the world.

THE EMPTY GRAVE OF ZSA ZSA GABOR

MATTHEW ZAPRUDER

On the radio I heard
that inimitable accent
say I vant to die
where I was born,
I remember her
so long ago
appearing on certain
Friday nights
as I religiously wasted
my youth watching
others embark
the boat of love,
rogues and ingenues
disappeared into
commercial breaks
unravaged then
into buffet light
emerged dazed
with a contentment
I have never felt,
some nights
she stepped
off the gangplank
so gracefully
stumbling a little,
one hand stretched
out to the dashing
purser, the other
holding the million
dollar nickel
of always about
to escape without

becoming a bride,
sometimes clad
in the white fur
attitude of a girl
from the Kremlin
who wouldn't talk
to one untouched
by evil, at others
under a blue hat,
a countess of
what could have been
were I not who I was,
she also appeared
perched amid
the luminous
Hollywood square
of afternoons
pretending not
to know facts
about outer space
or islands or headless
queens, her laughter
a sentient bell,
and never was
she until those last
days in the hospital
allowed to be
alone, then one
afternoon just as
she wished
her soul left
the body we all
desired and returned
to the old land,
wind came looking
but could not find her.

TEAM PLAYER

The cafeteria wall was pasted over with notices of the dead. Xeroxed photos of the missing and adverts for memorial services we, the survivors, were encouraged to attend. Every night for a week I'd been coming home from a different wake. Most of the deceased I'd met only a handful of times. "Why bother?" my wife asked me. "You think they'll give you a raise?"

This was before we split up. From the front desk of a Marriott, my wife was the second person I'd called to inform I was alive. The first call had gone out to my ex-wife, who'd started weeping, bless her, the moment she heard my voice. Her sobbing set my heart at ease. My second wife had said: "I knew you were okay because it always takes you so long to find parking on Tuesdays."

After the daylong trek up to my apartment, I made my third and last call of the day, to Nina's number. A girl picked up. She sounded a lot like Nina, only without an accent. I told her I was a friend from work.

"Have you heard from my mother?" Her nose seemed stuffed up.

"I thought I'd ask you the same question." I tried to make my voice bright. I could hear the booming sound of the day's news behind her. "Is anyone with you?"

Her father was at a medical conference. He'd called from the airport where the planes were all grounded. "She hasn't been answering her BlackBerry."

"My phone isn't working either," I said, as if bad reception were our biggest problem at the moment. "All the phone lines below Battery Park are down." She said she had to go. She didn't want to keep the phone busy in case her mother was trying to call the home line. "You'll let me know when she gets through," I said, no longer sure which of us was still doing the pretending.

For three weeks I'd been searching for Nina's name on the cafeteria wall, ever since I'd reported to our Midtown office, now the company headquarters. I won't divulge the name of my employer except to say it was a Prestigious Financial Services firm much in the news at that time. I'd counted 314 names so far, Nina's not among them. The nation blamed the terrorists, but I blamed Ericsson, my supervisor. It was the job of every group manager to collect and coordinate information about our fallen colleagues. This was the language used. I wondered if the omission had something to do with Nina being an overpaid consultant instead of a full-fledged drone like me. I found myself unable to raise the question with Ericsson, worried he would see me as a challenger to his authority or, worse, a competitor in grief.

The Company, it should be noted, took our grief seriously. The acre of IT cubicles where I sat—raised up like tents in a refugee camp—was around the corner from a corridor of executive offices, which had been handed over to the grief counselors brought in to tend to us. Around 1:00 p,m. the corridor would fill up with the lunchtime crowd, chatting while they stood in line for their twenty-five minutes of therapy. Most were Midtowners who'd been nowhere near the North Tower during the attack, and their grief had a boisterous quality, like that of young bathers who'd reveled in the flash chill of the ocean before jogging back to the safety of sand. My appointment was at two. I waited my turn behind two young female analysts from the upper floors.

"I told the client to think of it as a 25 percent sale on stock," a tall one said. "But they want to wait till we're, like, Filene's Basement."

"Some people need help seeing the upside," said her friend. Despite their different sizes, they wore the identical uniforms of early fall: snug black slacks, bright sleeveless tops.

"Everything's changed though. There's no going back from this," said the first woman.

"Maybe that's not such a bad thing. Let's face it, things couldn't just keep going the way they were going."

I felt myself buoyed by hope as I listened to them. The young can still change the world, I thought.

"Like these crazy hours they've been making all the analysts work," the woman continued. "I mean, it's just not sustainable."

A therapist came out. Not mine. "Clarice?"

"That's me!" said the first girl.

"Good luck!" her friend called after her.

My grief therapist's name was Marie. She had a smooth, freckled face and a shaky voice that made her sound elderly—though she was probably in her early fifties, like me—or fragile, like someone who'd entered the field because of her own needs for restoration. As usual, I spoke of my frustration with Ericsson.

"Why do you think you haven't asked him about posting a notice about your friend?"

"He doesn't like us bringing up the past."

Marie blinked three times, which she did whenever something I thought was obvious perplexed her.

"He doesn't like my talking about anything Nina and I did before the tragedy," I elaborated. I explained that my job was to finish building a new database system for the Company—the one Nina had been contracted to design. My manager's duty, on the other hand, was to maintain the company's bug-riddled existing database. A conflict of interest, since Nina's system, though incomplete, was considerably superior. The trouble was that the upper management who'd greenlit it, who understood its value to the Company, were all toast now. "I'm stranded in a sea of ignorance!" I complained.

"In times of crisis, people often want to stick to routine, to keep a footing on the familiar. Is there a way that understanding this might be helpful for you?" She smiled to encourage my agreement. She was trying to attribute to benign inertia what was better explained by animal territorialism. I was surprised that a therapist with whom people share their most disgusting secrets would encourage such a congenial view of humanity.

"If all of this happened on 10/11," I said, "I'd be in much better shape."

A discordance crept into Marie's doll-like features. "I hear your frustration." She sounded like a customer-service rep. It struck me that this was why the grief counselors had been brought in to begin with—to absorb our frustrations with the Company's pretragedy dysfunction, which the tragedy had borne open. "Have you thought of calling up Nina's family yourself?"

I agreed to call. To take, in Marie's words, a more active role in my bereavement. I wanted her to think I was making progress.

The engineers in my database group were dead. The company had halted all new hires so for the time being Ericsson made it one of my duties to check the state of maintenance jobs that ran nightly on the database computers. I explained that I'd been hired as an architect, not a technician, but Ericsson had puckered his bearded face and given me the usual speech. "We're all in this boat together. I shouldn't need to tell you how to rejuggle your priorities." The computers sat in the basement in an air-conditioned room we called the meat locker. I took the elevator down and resurfaced six hours later to headlights lurching in the boreal mist, and a message on my Nokia from Nina's daughter, inviting me to a gathering that evening for Nina. I checked my watch, feeling the crush of poor timing. The gathering had started two hours earlier. My Nokia still open, I punched in the number to call with my condolences. It went straight to voicemail, the girl's.

At home my wife was asleep in our bed, delicately snoring. Exhaustion knocked behind my eyes, but I found myself unable to get in beside her. No insult stings the sleepless like another's slumber. I went into the living room and turned on the TV. Someone was dead from anthrax spores mailed in a regular envelope. Crop dusters were being investigated as a means of dispersion. All of it—the anthrax, the shaky stock market, the attacks on our soil—was a test by those who wished to break our spirits. I reclined on the sectional and muted the volume, took from my fleece's pocket the recorder I'd kept there all day. It was a Sony, beige and just a little longer than an antique lighter. I regarded it in the dying light of the LCD display, then plugged my headphones in and let the rumble of Nina's voice fill my ears. It was a conversation from some time in my third week on the job, when I'd asked about the database's name.

"Why PIKE?" The world of IT was full of silly-sounding acronyms, but Parallel Integration Knowledge Encoding was a truly baffling one.

"It's a wish-granting factory." I could hear the smile in her voice. "The traders, the clients—they come to us with their requirements, all their little wishes, and PIKE makes them come true."

"You mean like the old folktale? The fisherman, his wife, and the goldfish."

"Gold*en* fish, not goldfish."

"Ah, it's a pike! Clever."

Clevurr. I'd never been able to de-Russify my *r*s. I felt a belated sensation of embarrassment on account of my accent, so much thicker than hers, and a fresh embarrassment at how I'd hidden my recordings from Nina, keeping the Sony inside my trouser pocket, sometimes glancing at it involuntarily. Once she asked what I was looking for. I blushed and told her I'd recently quit smoking, that my fingers were still reaching for cigarettes I no longer carried. The transparency of my lie made me angry at her. Wasn't it Nina's job to document her work? To make the reasoning behind her code comprehensible to whoever took over for her? She'd opted to skip all the boring, uncompensated work of annotating her code in her hurry to build the system. Once her contract was over, I'd have to pry apart the whole design, reverse her steps like a plumber, following the convoluted logical pipes beneath PIKE's processes. I'd inquired if I could record her responses. Nina gave it some thought but, in the end, refused. I suspected she was skeptical of revealing the hidden patterns of her genius. I chalked it up to an Eastern-European suspicion of surveillance. Who knows what parts of ourselves we surrender when we open our mouths?

I waited another two days before calling Nina's daughter. "I'm sorry I couldn't attend the gathering."

"Who is this?"

I reminded her.

"Only one person came," she said.

"To the wake?"

"No, not to the wake." She didn't sound outraged at my question, though. "One person came from Mom's work."

"Who?" I asked.

"I think maybe it was her manager?"

I felt a spasm in my chest. "The heavyset one, with the gray ponytail?"

"That's him."

I had no memory of Ericsson mentioning Nina's memorial to me. Did he think it unworthy of my attention?

"Have there been any… developments?" I wondered then what other information Ericsson had not bothered to share.

"No, they're still looking." Her voice sounded not so much discouraged as hollowed out of hope.

"It's early yet," I said.

I was picturing those bucket brigades with their dogs, combing through the rubble for wedding rings and laminated IDs. I wanted to ask her what it was she hoped they'd find.

"My dad sent her toothbrush to the medical examiner," she said then.

Without wanting to I pictured Nina's dental work, the crude zinc fillings of her Polish childhood. I still can't explain what grabbed hold of me in that moment, what rush of largesse prompted me to offer her daughter a piece of my bounty. "If you'd like, I have something of your mother's," I said.

"What? What is it?" Her adolescent voice lifted an octave, like a child I'd teased with an early birthday present.

"Just some recordings of her voice on a project. Mostly technical."

"Oh."

"If you aren't interested..."

"I am!" She repeated it several times "I am, I am. I'm interested."

I promised I'd get them to her the following week.

In the meantime our cemetery-like cafeteria was growing livelier by the day. The Wall of Grief was no longer a place for trafficking intelligence about the dead, but gossip about the living. Who'd been promoted from analyst to associate. Who had made VP overnight. Beneath the patchy mood of grief one could feel the ecstatic pulse of ambition. Opportunism abhors a vacuum, I thought as I watched them chatter among themselves. "Take a look at these grave robbers," said Yuri, an IT consultant who'd started sharing Newports with me on the curb after my therapy. I had taken up smoking again. I suspected Yuri might have liked to rob a grave himself if he'd been something other than a lowly contractor with an accent even thicker than mine.

The big news of the week was that our Company's one surviving director had appeared on a financial news program. He'd been the youngest, at thirty-six, of the five. What little I knew about him included the fact that he rode a Kawasaki Vulcan to work and wore his bomber jacket on Fridays. The loss of his fellow directors had put a halo around his head and given him unheard of executive reach inside the Company. On TV he'd spoken about how the firm was more united than ever to meet our clients' needs. We would not only persevere but come out of this tragedy stronger. Yuri and I both agreed the speech had probably kept our stock price from collapsing.

"Check out that one?" Yuri gestured at a network technician we both knew. "Cal the Cowboy. Last week he was in a polo shirt and saggy jeans. Now the guy owns a suit and tie." The only times I'd seen Cal in the North Tower were when he'd slouched up from Midtown to swap out a faulty piece of hardware. In his new suit he stood straighter, like the final figure in man's chain of evolution.

"Maybe he wore it to one of the wakes at St. Patrick's and thought it suited him," I suggested.

I hadn't intended it as a joke, but Yuri sounded amused. "That's good," he said. "Won't take off his funeral suit. Thinks he's a regular Jackie Kennedy."

That evening I told my wife about Cal the Cowboy, tried to make his upgrade sound amusing. She'd cooked us a nice meal. We opened a wine. She'd been treating me with delicacy ever since failing to weep at my continued existence. We were keeping the conversation light, talking about the decline in road accidents, a return to civility, while she absently studied the phone bill. I told her about Cal and his new suit. "Well, good for him," she said finally. "Today he wears the suit, tomorrow he is the suit."

"Come on. The guy's a technician," I said. "A janitor."

"You talk about his jacket, and what about your shoes? You ever plan to get them cleaned off?" I had worn those shoes the day of the tragedy, and they were still in the back of my closet, coated in ash. "What's this number?" she said, showing me the bill. I silently debated whether to tell her I'd spoken with Nina's daughter. Everything in our lives was separate—separate children, separate checking accounts—but we were on the same phone plan. There was no point keeping secrets. "I've spoken with Nina's family." I confessed. Her brow tensed slightly. "Your boss the Polish lady?"

"She wasn't my boss," I said. "They're desperate to find anything of hers in that rubble. I'm going to send them the recordings."

"You already promised?"

"Can you imagine what it's like to have someone you love disappear into nothing?"

"Always acting in haste. You said she didn't like you to record her. What if it gets back to the Company?"

"Why would her daughter give them to anyone there?" I said.

She studied me. "You mean you only spoke with the girl, not the father?"

I could sense her disappointment in my inability to see things through. I assured her I was the only one who knew the guts of the new system. I was indispensable. "It's because you're the only one who knows that that pig will try to replace you first." I assumed she was talking about Ericsson. "No one wants to be beholden to the past, honey."

Later that night, flushed with wine, she asked if I was coming to bed. "In a little bit." I told her I still had work to do and went to my desk to listen to Nina's voice. Much of our talk was technical, though not all. We often took our conversation into lunch, and that night, replaying one of the MP3 files I'd uploaded, I could hear the clanging of dishes behind us, snatches of Vietnamese at a cafe we went to, where Nina liked to talk about Agatha Christie. "If the book is under 55,000 words, the murderer is certainly a woman; over 70,000, it's a man." She'd done a statistical analysis of Christie's books in graduate school, for fun. At her suggestion, I'd bought a copy of *The Murder at the Vicarage*. "You're *sure* it's a man?" I teased

"Is the road they travel on land or water?"

"Ah, so you don't remember."

"Land. Then unquestionably a man."

In the spaces between her words, I could hear the wince of pleasure as Nina inhaled the pho into which she liked to pump an absurd amount of hoisin sauce. Would I have taken notice of her had I not known her? A middle-aged executive with blonde hair and glasses, a few extra pounds on her frame from the limitless hours she billed. But I *had* known her. The recordings had preserved all the charm of her voice, which was British inflected, the Polish accent deeply buried under years of tutoring. Her English teacher had been the one who'd hooked her on Agatha Christie. Years later she could still retrieve hundreds of complicated plots, just as she could easily parse thousands of lines of code. I let the percolations of her voice wash over me again. How eerily soothing to hear her fretting about our delivery schedule, unconscious of the coming storm. I heard her BlackBerry buzzing on the tape. It was her daughter. "Milena," she said apologetically and took the call.

I knew my wife was right: if Ericsson got hold of the recordings, I'd be fired on the spot. And I was the only one who could keep PIKE alive. "They're almost ready," I told Milena when she called me back about the tapes. Her next call, a week later, I let go to voicemail. I couldn't explain to her that it was her mother's work I wished to protect—her legacy!

"I'm still having the dream," I told Marie.

I felt like I was spending my nights being chased, running from the same dust cloud I'd escaped when I'd dragged my legs down Liberty Street to the Seaport and clicked my car door open a few moments before the cannonball of ash covered the block in white.

"It must be terrifying to come within an inch of your life," Marie said.

I had in mind to ask if she'd gotten her license from a cereal box. "This isn't about that. It's because I'm running out of time!" I'd seen Ericsson go into his meetings with the new managers, youngsters ready to start from scratch and make names for themselves. I worried he would persuade them that PIKE was no longer suitable for the Company. People at the bottom, like me, might know how systems work, I said, but it's the ones at the top who know how to work the system.

"I'm concerned," Marie said. "That the issues you bring up would be better addressed by HR. The purpose of grief therapy is to process your feelings about the recent events."

"You want me to talk about my feelings? Alright," I said. "My father had a wife and two children before the war, all of them killed by Nazis while he was on the front. After the war he went back to look for them, but no one in his town knew what happened to them. He couldn't find a single person who'd even heard of their names. Like they'd never existed."

Beneath the corporate agitprop about all of us being in one boat, I understood that our department was in the throes of a turf war and that I was running out of time. The few hours I had to work each day on PIKE were eaten into by progress reports and triaging of the old system. Ericsson had started requiring that I submit every block of code to Quality Assurance for testing. Over my shoulder he peered at the procedures I showed him as if he was looking for an actual bug to squash. "Send it over to QA before you write any more." The delay tactic of a man afraid of becoming obsolete.

I went to find Yuri, who'd said he knew a Russian tester in QA. Quality Assurance was a strictly Soviet operation, meaning you could jump the queue if you found a friend on the inside. "No problem, this guy will run any test you want, put his signature on your code," Yuri said in his street junkies's voice. He could see from my face I was dubious. "No strings attached." He looked insulted. "We have to stick together, look around." We'd walked to the deli counter. Among the funereal perks of our revamped cafeteria was an excellent smoked meats section.

He had a valid point, I thought. I could see the Filipinos huddled at their own table, the Chinese programmers had theirs by the windows. The Indians were split along the usual caste lines of homegrowns and H1-imports. I hadn't been with the company long enough to know how much mixing went on to begin with. All the ethnics looked more wary to me, less energized by the tragedy than the native-born with their gift of gab. "He's treating you like a consultant-slave," Yuri said when I confessed my own troubles with Ericsson. Yuri was a self-described consultant slave himself ("no voice, just two hands and a tongue for licking ass"), his slave driver a woman he called Barracuda who humiliated him by docking his smoke breaks. "There's no way I can finish on schedule if I don't bring in code from my old jobs," I confessed. The only way to use the work from my old jobs was to load the code onto the Company network. "Don't ask Ericsson's permission," Yuri said. "He's gonna cite the Policy." Out of deference to security and legality, we had to build all our code internally. A policy followed to the letter except for all the times it was overruled by higher-ups. "Who can you get to override? Who's your dotted-line guy?" Yuri had no dotted-line guy, no one to crawl to who could pull rank over Barracuda. I couldn't think of anyone. There were deep craters in management all the way to the top. "What about the Bomber Jacket?" he suggested.

"Too high."

"In a flood seek the highest hill."

Getting an official meeting with Bomber Jacket proved complicated now that he was in meetings all day or on the news. Our stock price was being closely watched, an indicator of the health of the economy and the tenacity of the American spirit. In the men's room I'd heard him giving a journalist a quote about crisis as an opportunity for change. He didn't bother to hang up before flushing.

It was at the urinals that I finally made my approach. He had his phone in one hand, his pecker in the other, shaking off the last drops. I introduced myself as he zipped up. "You can see I'm busy." His phone was squeezed between his shoulder and ear; he kept right on talking into it as I followed him to his office. "You have two minutes before my next call," he said. I told him about the company's expensive investment in PIKE, before the tragedy.

"I don't need a financial report."

"I'd like to speed along our timeline. I've been working on the new system at night, from home."

"Why can't you do your work at work?"

"With respect, sir, we're all scrambling to keep the ship afloat," I said, quoting Ericsson. "I heard your speech on CNBC," I added. "You said you wanted to make this company even better than before. Adapt to the future. I believe in this also. Why I came to you and no one else."

He studied me, gauging my sincerity or stupidity. In college, in Saint Petersburg, we'd all been required to take a course in scientific socialism. You could write gibberish on your papers, but as long as you added, "I want to contribute to the Collective," they were not allowed to fail you. "A one-time exception," the Bomber Jacket said. "Haul it all in at once. I don't want to go through this drill again."

Nina's daughter called me later that afternoon from a number I didn't recognize. "I was wondering if you were able to get those recordings?" She sounded shy, like she'd been working up the nerve to call.

"Yes, yes!" I said, as if suddenly remembering. I had in fact loaded up all the recordings on the computer and spent my evenings wondering what to cut and keep. "I'm still looking," I said. "There are so many MP3 files to go through."

"You said that last time."

"I know. I've been busy. I want to get them to you," I insisted. "I need just a little more time. You understand?"

It sounds insincere now, but it was not merely to make myself essential that I set out on this path. It really was for Nina. Her obituary had finally appeared on the Wall of Grief. It described her love of travel, of ballroom dance, and referred to a recent family trip through eastern Europe. "She was the ideal travel companion," her husband Otto was quoted saying. "She packed everything, from sunblock to the maps we'd need to carry." Maps! I thought. Did anyone care what Stravinsky's favorite soft drink was? Or if Einstein made his goddamned bed? I would let her work live on.

I was moving along swiftly now and reporting on PIKE's progress directly to the Bomber Jacket. Ericsson, naturally, was not happy about my going over his head, but the most he could do was to keep pushing back the date of the migration to the new system and punish me by making me write daily reports. Every evening, I watched him eyeball them in his cubicle and throw them in the trash.

Finally, the only thing there was left to do was run the two systems side by side, comparing inputs and outputs. The process would involve the whole team and take a week. "Let's set a date," I told Ericsson.

"I can't spare people. We've got everyone on three different jobs already."

"If that asshole's trying to bottleneck you," said Yuri, "then you've got to show him who's the boss and who's the asshole."

This was, incidentally, the punchline to Yuri's favorite joke. All the organs of the body are arguing over who's boss. The brain declares himself the master planner. The muscles say without them the body would be lying on the couch all day. The stomach insists on his supremacy because he feeds everyone. And all the while the asshole's squeaking its little tune: *I'm the boss, I'm the boss.* The other organs laugh at him until he gets so ticked off he squeezes himself shut. You know the rest. The joke had a variety of meanings for Yuri depending on his mood. Sometimes it meant simply that you didn't need to be the brain to be the boss, just an asshole. But some days it took on a more subtle meaning, which was that even the lowliest employee could pull a power move by creating a little unexpected congestion. "Disruption is the only way to be taken seriously, comrade," he said.

The answer presented itself to me a week later in Nina's tapes. I'd been asking about the weaknesses of the system PIKE was supposed to replace. The biggest vulnerability was, predictably, the size of queue memory. "How many trades at a time is the system scaled for?" I heard myself ask on tape.

"One twenty, max. But it never happens. We don't normally get more than sixty trades at a time."

"And what would happen if you did?"

"Same thing as if there are too many customers trying to push to the front of the cashier's window. Errors." The system would slow to a crawl.

"And what would you do then?" I said.

"Put up an out-of-service sign and build a bigger register."

"You mean increase the size of the disk the log writes to, and start everything up again?"

"Sure… according to the manual." Whenever Nina brought up "the manual" I knew she'd looked under the hood and found another solution. I fast-forwarded the tape and listened to her explain how she'd added memory dynamically during a jam without ever having to shut down the system and lose the existing trades. There it was: an inevitable blockage only I could relieve to show who was who. My very own bottleneck.

I began to neglect my duties, no longer running the tests I'd done before. Letting maintenance jobs pile up. The market was a choppy sea, its volatility causing our clients to trade compulsively, to order and dump stock in spurts. Left long enough, these delays could create a disruption. A disruption would create a crisis. A crisis, an opportunity!

The gentler part of my nature bristled at this sabotage by neglect. I felt like a doctor failing to run a stress test on a cardiac patient with two clogged arteries who thinks he's alright as long as he can swing a golf club. But I was no doctor. I had no Hippocratic oath to break.

"Every new order is built on carnage," I told Marie at our next appointment.

"Would you like to talk about your father?" She suggested. I obliged her. "He refused to come with me to America, to start from scratch. Made a big deal about wanting to be buried with his first family then died alone."

"You said you two had a troubled relationship."

I didn't remember saying that, but I must have said many mixed-up things in my grief. She'd fixate on the parents, of course. "The only thing my father hated more than when I lost to him at chess," I said, "was when I won."

Marie nodded sympathetically.

"He wasn't a bad man, just a sick one. He lost his whole family in the war."

My father had been a difficult, angry man, driven mad by the losses. The only respite from his rages came in our occasional chess games. By twelve I'd begun to beat him, but if I won too fast, he would spend the evening sulking. I learned to calibrate my victories, to weave weak moves into what might have been shining games.

"And do you feel like you'll be punished again, if you advocate for yourself more directly?" I wasn't sure what she meant by *advocate for yourself*.

"I was an only child, but he took no pleasure in my face," I said.

It was around this time that I received my final call from Milena. "I don't know why you'd tell me you had my mom's voice on those tapes when you obviously don't!"

It made me feel aggravated to be accused like this. "But I do have them!" I pleaded. "I wouldn't lie to you. I'm almost done. I can give you everything this week."

Even if Ericsson got his hands on them now, it would be too late. PIKE would swim.

"You'll email them to me?"

"I'd rather not. I don't want to pass any sensitive information on an open network."

"You said you took all that out."

"Can I give you the drive in person?" I asked. I knew suddenly that this was what I'd been waiting to ask her all along. To get a final look at Nina on a new face. "There's a Vietnamese restaurant downtown, easy to get to." I gave her the address.

A couple of days later I arrived at my desk after lunch and found people inside Ericsson's cubicle: the manager from the Applications group, Cal the technician, and the Bomber Jacket all crowded around the keyboard. I heard the competing birdsongs of their mobiles, all going unanswered. "Where have you been?" Ericsson demanded.

"What's the trouble?"

"The log fool condition, the database can't record what it's doing."

"Alright, I'll take a look," I said. I waited for him to get up.

Bomber Jacket picked up his call. It was the head of the trading desk. The traders couldn't put in their trades. The business was stalled.

"How many trades were in the queue when the delay began?" I asked.

The Bomber Jacket spoke from behind me. "Eighty million." He had no use for our jargon. He talked in the language of money: the amount of the day's mounting losses.

"I'll take a look," I said. I had rehearsed this moment.

"You were supposed to run the stress tests last week," Ericsson announced loudly.

"It's your system. I didn't configure this thing, and I didn't size it. Did you check the manual?"

"Yeah, I looked at it."

He knew if he shut it down now, we'd lose the trades. He didn't want blood on his hands. Didn't want to be the scalp the company presented to the board.

"There might be another way to solve it," I said.

"The book said to shut it down," said Ericsson, covering his bases.

I felt something unexplainable roiling inside me, the long tumbling despair wanting to rupture like a cloud of hot debris. "So why haven't you? You been waiting for me to show up and pull the trigger?"

"Let's all take it easy," said the Bomber Jacket. He put a hand on my shoulder as I sat down. "You said you knew how to do this," he reminded me. His hand was still on my clavicle, encouraging me. He was giving me a chance to fix things. To be indispensable.

It took me seventeen minutes to shift the transaction logs to another disk while the system continued running. The equivalent, as Nina had explained to me, of moving the customer line outside the store. I heard the collective groan of relief when the trades began to run, the exhalation of the pardoned.

"Alright, what are we waiting for, champagne?" Bomber Jacket said happily. "Everyone back to their desks."

No *nice work*. No *thank you*s. The company had bled no money and felt no pain. It was then that a sudden weariness overtook me. I had fixed one problem, and there would be some other, smaller, problem next week. As long as I kept fixing things the migration to PIKE would be delayed. It occurred to me that I had failed Nina's memory in the most enormous of ways. That the opportunity for such grand disaster might never present itself again.

What can I say of the following day? I remember the cloud cover was low and the snow fell in thick wet clumps, refusing to stick to the cobblestones on Water Street where I waited for Milena to enter the cafe. It was January now and I hadn't been inside the pho place since early September. It seemed both miraculous and appalling to me that nothing inside had changed—the same beige and blue tiled floor, the same hanging menu of near identical soups. I sat beside the cold window, the flash drive tucked away in my breast pocket.

I recognized him as soon as he entered. Pale blue eyes sunk behind expensive frames. A black overcoat with the collar turned up like Napoleon. When he approached me, his balding forehead looked patched from the cold. "You're the one who's been talking to my daughter?"

I spoke my name and asked if he wanted to sit. He gave the place a look, as if searching for hidden traps. "You can't talk to my kid anymore," he repeated.

"You have been upsetting her. If you do it again, I'll have to—" He couldn't finish the thought. Whatever threats he'd rehearsed on his way must have sounded foolish to him once he'd seen me. Whatever I'd expected—another glimpse of Nina in a different face, to be cocooned once more in the obliviousness of the past—all that was foolish, too. I took the flash drive from my pocket and set it down between us. "This is for your daughter," I said. "For both of you."

Otto stared at it as if it were covered with stomach acid.

"This is your gift? Her mother talking to a strange man?"

"It's a side of Nina she might want to know later."

"What side?"

"Her commitment to her work."

"Her work?" He scoffed. "Nina didn't care about her work. All she cared about was her paycheck. Clocking her hours. I said I'd buy her a cappuccino machine, but she said she liked to drink from the one at the office. Two sips and out the door. And you?" He turned his chlorine gaze on me. "What's your excuse?"

I'd learned to dread this question. "I couldn't find parking," I said.

He clutched the device and slipped it into his coat pocket. "I know my wife. She would not have allowed someone to record her." There was bitterness in his words, but not in his face. He squeezed his shoulders in a kind of farewell shrug, as if all of this—our talk, his threats—were perfectly ridiculous. I watched him walk outside, the snow falling into his open collar.

When I returned to the office the Bomber Jacket called me in. "I'll need your badge," he said.

"The problems existed long before I came on board," I said.

He winced. "The trouble is, you're just not a team player."

I knew that I had let my chance slip away. The bottleneck had been Nina's gift to me, but I had been too timid, playing the hero instead of letting the old system sink so her golden fish could swim. "With all due respect, sir," I said, "my team is dead."

My computer was shut down by the time I returned to my cubicle. A cardboard box sat on my desk, it's flaps open. I didn't bother to pack it. I left the room, and then the building, taking my place among the departed.

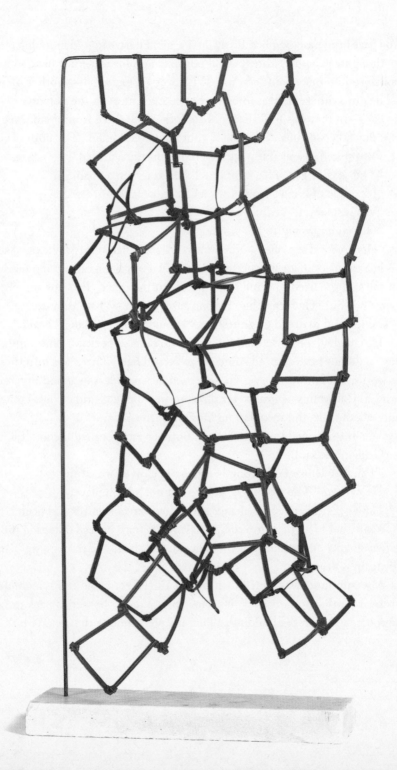

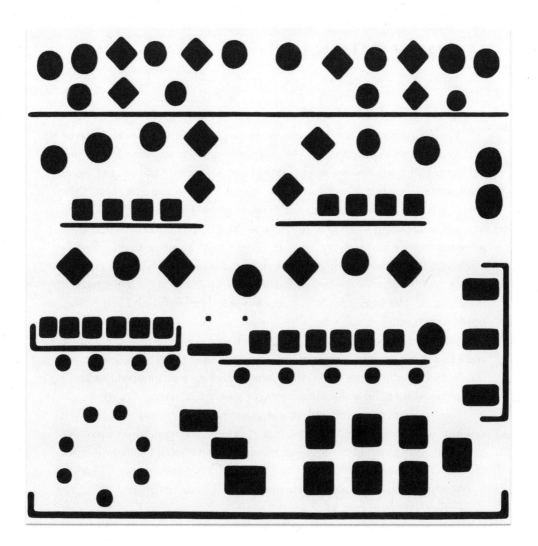

Matt Magee

HONEYSUCKLE

I can almost see it.

A barely controlled environment. Some paths through the woods, layered with cedar chips. A gazebo on a cliff overlooking a stream. Patches of open field, sticky with wildflowers and hovering bees. My mother and a man I didn't know, sitting on a bench that was overwhelmed with vines and creepers, their four hands clasped in a knot between them, praying. The place smelled sweet, like perfume, except when you got close to the orange plastic bags that were mounted on wire frames every fifty feet like the markers along a hiking trail—those smelled acid-sweet, like rancid cheese, a scent I'd never experienced before, revolting and somehow tantalizing. I couldn't stop daring myself to breathe it in. The bags were full of decomposing beetles floating in a putrid, heavy, brown water.

The place was called Mustard Seeds—there was a sign—and my mother and I had come here for a reason, though I no longer remembered what this reason was. Maybe I hadn't been told. I know the visit was important to her—crucial. She'd been sad and sometimes angry for weeks. For months. My whole life. She and my father didn't look at each other, not if they could help it. When one entered a room, the other one exited. There was something she'd get here—this I understood without her telling me—that would somehow solve the crisis that was her life.

Mustard Seeds. The place was strong with religious sentiment.

Earlier, that morning, when we'd arrived.

There'd been a visitor center or a gift shop, maybe. A rustic building. And the man unlocked the door and turned on the light. He let me wander around looking at things. The usual religious souvenirs: posters and place mats with Bible verses superimposed over peaceful scenes of nature, matchstick crosses, footprints posters, greeting cards, crèches carved from marbled wood, crèches lodged inside snow globes, molded plastic animals lined up two by two, candles in the shape of crosses and fishes, posters of dirty kids with gigantic eyes, a film of dust layered over all of it.

On a shelf in a corner, a few inches off the floor, a stack of comic books. I liked comic books. My mom had let me buy one once, *The Micronauts*, about tiny machine men who did battle in outer space against much larger, much meaner machine men. I'd read it so many times the cover had come off, the pages strained and bulged against the staples.

"You can stay here and look at those if you want while your mom and I have our talk," the man said. His voice was even, eerie and calming. Everything about him, his tight blond beard, his thinning hair, the nubby brown socks peeking out of his sandals, evoked the sense of a benevolent shepherd.

He and my mother left me alone in that dark dusty room and I leafed through the comic books.

One in particular, I remember, about Coach Tom Landry and the Dallas Cowboys. The team had no discipline, no sense of mission. They were a bunch of misfits, criminals, crack ups. Landry came to them in his gray suit and fedora and he told them the Good News. There was something more to life than squabbling and cursing and brawling and thieving. If they let themselves be saved, he would save their team. He'd take them to the Super Bowl. He and Jesus Christ would lead them to salvation. And they prayed together and they broke bread together and together they achieved all the things he'd promised, humbly, as a team, the single superstar among them, Jesus Christ.

I must have grown bored with the visitor center because later I was outside, still clutching the comic book, digging with my foot at a cedar path that ran along the edge of a stream. I could see the man. I could see my mother. They were next to each other on that wooden bench, on a different path from mine, higher up, on a cliff jutting over the edge of the stream. A place I couldn't and knew I shouldn't reach. My mother was crying.

It was hot outside, but dry, one of those days people sometimes call perfect.

The sunlight seemed alive. It had weight and dimension. Long yellowy cylinders shooting through the leafy treetops. Splotches of golden brightness, like translucent disco balls, soft and yielding, filled with flecks of glitter. They hovered and floated and coaxed me into the shadows along the riverbank.

It wasn't just the balls of light floating around me. Everything else seemed richer and crisper than usual as well. The darkness of the shadows was a black beyond black. The waxy teardrop leaves of the weeds near the water seemed to breathe, rising and falling and quivering. The mulch on the ground consisted of an uncountable number of shades of brown and orange and I could see each one distinct and isolated from the others. Flies zigged in and out of the light, flashing the steely green, red, and blue armor of their torsos. Bullfrogs—I could hear them more than I could see them—sometimes I caught a splash just after they were gone. The air smelled piney, watery, like fresh dirt—scents lapping over me, swirling together.

I stayed on my path. I was a good little boy, aware of my obligation on this day to not get lost, to not cause trouble. My mommy needed me to be good. I had to remember that. It was important.

But when the stream turned and the path turned with it, I couldn't stop following the glittery balls of light. I had to see what was next. Even if this meant losing sight of my mom and the weird shepherd man way up on the ledge. I wasn't really walking anyway. Walking required intention. I was more gliding through the landscape of my senses. I'd crossed some boundary in my perception and now I was seeing things for what they were, not just as the names I'd attached to them, but as forms and colors and sounds, smells and textures. The world around me seemed to exist in some perfect, natural equilibrium, and I imagined that what I was experiencing now was what God had experienced on the first day.

A slight rise, the water moving faster. Wind chimes to my left. Honeycomb skins of lichen on the boulders there.

And then the shadows abruptly came to an end and the light rushed down in front of me, all together, all at once. It seemed to concentrate in a solid mass, a glass house illuminated from the inside, filled with warmth and a bright pool of grass gone to seed. I broke through the plane, out of the shadows and into all this light. I swam into the field up to my waist. A tree had come loose in the soft earth. It lay on its side, half-submerged in the tall grass, its root system exposed and splayed toward the sky. That perfume I'd smelled earlier, sweet and sugary. A whole mess of bees taking turns at the white trumpet-shaped flowers on the vines curled around the lower reaches of the roots. I followed the scent. It was strong enough to taste.

The flowers. Honeysuckle, I later found out. If the bees liked them, I figured, I would too. I picked one. A thick sap collected at its base. I touched it to my tongue. A faintly lavender, watery sweetness. I sucked at the flower until the taste was gone. Then I picked another one and sucked again. An addictive taste.

Each time it faded, I wanted it back. I sucked and sucked at the honeysuckle and my eyes began to tear and I rubbed them and sucked some more and rubbed my eyes some more—they itched from somewhere deep inside the ducts—and I sucked some more flowers and then I was blind. A film of what felt like hair had grown over my eyeballs, prickly like nettles, gooey like Jell-O. I touched my face to feel for what was going on. It was like pillows had been shoved under my skin. My body had come alive, separate from me. It was rising up and squeezing, trying to push me out.

I let loose a trill of confusion and fear.

I sank into the grass—I could hear it rustling, a torrent, all around me—and I clawed at my eyes.

And she was right there, my mother, wrapping me up in her not-yet chubby arms, crying over me, and the shepherd was there too—I could hear him talking, calm, unflappable, about allergens and hospitals and his car just up the way.

And this is what I remember most from that day: She'd been in a fragile state; I'd been supposed to be quiet and self-contained, just for a few hours, until she was done meeting with the Mustard Seed man; I had a responsibility to her; I was stronger than her—I was supposed to be stronger than her on that day; without me she was lost. And there I was with my fear and my honeysuckle-puffed face, betraying her. *Be bold, be brave, don't be afraid of anything, for I, the Lord your God, am with you always.* As I bit my lip and held my breath, as the tears convulsed inside me and caught in my throat, I prayed. Not for me, but for her. Whatever happened next would be all my fault.

Then I was in the air, still in her arms, and we were rushing toward the car and I was screaming. The Dallas Cowboys. Tom Landry. "The comic book. I dropped it. Where is it?"

"It's right here," she said. "Everything's going to be okay. You can have it when we get to the hospital."

I don't know if that was true or not, but later, when my eyes cleared and I asked to see it, she couldn't find it.

In the weeks after that day, when, alone in the shadows of our damp tract house, I wondered if my father was ever coming home, I'd think about the comic book and feel a panicky ache in my chest. I'd want to ask her what had happened to it. I didn't though. I didn't want to burden her. I was enough of a pest already.

SIX MONTHS

I.   After seven years together, Mona told Liesel she should go ahead and leave, if leaving was what she wanted to do. They sat across from each other at the small Formica table they had purchased from a kitsch fair in Stepney Green, both moderately stunned by finality. To avoid Liesel's tears, and her ugly tendency to deny anyone else's emotions with the strength of her own, Mona looked left, out of the little window, to find the sun shining and plump rain falling in a manner that seemed cinematic and hopeful.

"Dying isn't much fun, you know." Liesel sniveled. "You *do* know, Mona. You've been here this whole time, so I know you understand. I need to be done now. I know you'll understand, eventually."

Mona couldn't respond to that. The clouds were really pulling focus, doing something balletic in the sky, and a slight ringing had begun in both her ears, like someone had hung up a phone in her head. Liesel had moved on to practicalities: Arrangements had been made, relationships brokered. In time, Mona was to expect a call from some black women who were part of a collective.

"They're great." Liesel added. "Queer, cool. I know you; don't dismiss them. They'll listen, okay? They'll understand."

"Understand what?"

Liesel began crying again. "Oh, honey," she said.

A few months later, Mona came home to find Liesel gone. She'd left behind a small maze of cardboard boxes in the living room, loudly addressed to herself c/o her father in Hamburg. A while ago, she had said: *If I address them to me, he'll know to open them only when he's ready*. Mona couldn't stand it. She relabeled them all, accurately. The following week a courier came to collect them.

Then, Mona was alone. She wore her silk sleep bonnet through breakfasts of steamed cabbage and saltfish with the little window in the kitchen shut. She talked to herself freely and loudly throughout the flat as she made Turkish coffee with the pot Liesel had haggled over in the Grand Bazaar, as she looked in the bathroom cabinet Liesel had fished out of a skip in Camberwell, while she took leisurely, potent shits on the toilet Liesel had insisted was haunted due to its spontaneous

THOMAS / A PUBLIC SPACE   73

habit of flushing by itself. She placed a star on the top of the Christmas tree and threw the punk fairy—a Barbie with torn tights and hair snipped into a mohawk that Liesel had worshipped as self-fashioned feminist iconography—in the bin. She threw the coffee pot and the bathroom cabinet in the bin.

A plumber came to fix the toilet. This plumber made a mundane and unnecessary racket, clanking spanners and pipes, while Mona perched on the edge of the bath aching to see a ghost. In a perilous twist on a cliché, the plumber's ass crack stretched out of her jeans, a gentle, downy slit. This caused Mona pain. The pain was unexpected, both searing and collapsing, and not unlike the imagined effects of drinking household bleach. Mona stood and teetered over the plumber; it had seemed easier to implode while seated.

"I'm a professional, you know. There's no need to watch," the plumber said.

"Calm down," Mona replied. "I'm not watching you."

A fresh Barbie arrived in the post. Mona had no clue what it was doing showing up like that, like it had something to proclaim. She threw it in the bin. Two women arrived at the door. Again, Mona was stumped. They'd been knocking and ringing for days, they said, for weeks. One wore a headwrap the color of the Blue Lagoon, the other a buzz cut and black skullcap. We're from round the corner, they said, your girlfriend—we're sorry—she told us about you, they said, we're here, they said, if you need us. Blue Lagoon handed Mona a card. This card had been cut out of a larger bit of card. It had a rainbow on it and the silhouette of a woman with a voluminous Afro. Mona had never met these women before. They seemed fine, but she had no idea who they were. After they left, the card sat on the Formica table for a while until she threw it in the bin. There were mementos, other maiming slithers of Liesel. Mona collected them all up from their hidey-holes and underbeds and evil spying corners, and she threw them all in the bin.

The nights had drawn in. After work, from the little window in the kitchen, all Mona could see were strips of warm light, the steady golden glow of preferable homes. She pecked a fork into oversize portions at the Formica table. She found herself contacting her mother, who lived in Port Antonio, more often than usual, hanging on in front of the laptop while in that other world beyond the screen visitors came and went, meat was chopped, mosquitoes killed, dogs shooed, floors were swept and pots washed, and life continued without her involvement.

"Mummy?" Mona sometimes said into that sun-drenched abyss. "Mummy?" But it was loud there and busy, as it always had been, and fairly often Mona wasn't heard.

"Are you listening?" Brigitte asked.

"I'm listening," Mona said.

Over brunch in Peckham, Brigitte had decided that Mona needed to get fucked, but Elke had decided it was much too soon. "What you probably need," Elke continued, "is just some companionship."

"That's what I'm doing here," Mona replied. "With you."

At brunch in Peckham a week later, Brigitte shot Elke a look. "Maybe you should move into a house share or something, Mona," she said. "For a while."

Mona's eggs were tasteless. Everything on her plate was either too wet or too dry, dry as ashes, and defiantly, conspicuously tasteless. "I'm thirty-five, Brigitte," she said.

"But social interaction is important." Elke was undeterred. "I don't mean to sound harsh, given the circumstances, but I think being in a relationship for a long time, you can become kind of codependent."

"Codependent?" Mona asked.

"Yeah, codependent, and then it's so hard, you know, when you've lost that person, to relate to other people easily." She took a breath. "I mean, we hadn't heard from you in months, and here you are at brunch. Again! You just need a refresher course."

"Also, I'm thirty-six," Brigitte added. "And I live in a house share."

Originally, these women had been Liesel's friends. Or friends of friends, maybe. Still, in the bath that afternoon, Mona considered what Elke had said. A refresher course in empathy? All right then. Liesel lurked behind steam on Mona's locked screen, still pink cheeked and winking. Lack of feeling and lack of understanding had been two of her recurrent complaints. Were they the same thing? Mona asked Liesel: "Are they? You know everything. Are they?" Pointless questioning had become part of Mona's ritual, along with the afternoon baths drawn at near-scalding temperature. Liesel's face would stare back familiar until it grew uncanny and then abstract, just like Mona's own body, dark and cryptid beneath the water.

II.   Mona offered to take the cat. Mrs. Howath, the neighbor, was going into a hospice, and her black cat wasn't welcome. Her daughter had slipped a note under the door: *Could you help? Mum would rather he went to a good home.* Mona didn't know if she counted, but the daughter didn't really seem to care that much. She scooped the passing animal up from the floor and thrust it into Mona's arms, machine gunning thanks. "You're so kind," she added, breathless. "Considering everything. A real star."

Mona took this, and the cat, away with her. Its name was George, and it looked at her blankly with jaundiced eyes. When she set it down on the linoleum, it stood there unmoving until Mona felt embarrassed and left the room. Then the daughter was at the door, still breathless. She had forgotten: "Food, toys, bowl. Sorry, I'm frantic. Here you go. Thanks again. You're an angel. Considering everything."

The bowl was fluorescent orange, and it had *George* embossed in black cursive on it. The cat eyed it as though it had never seen this bowl, never in its whole entire life.

"Go on, eat," Mona said, having filled the bowl to the brim. Facts were that she didn't really know what to do with the creature, she didn't particularly like cats, and she'd never once in her whole entire life considered owning one. George yawned then wandered out of the kitchen.

Cat appetite, animal adoption, adoption breakdown, empathy, empathy refresher course

Mona spent the rest of the day googling. Results were mixed. She decided it wasn't yet time to take decisive action. A text to Elke about George had gone unanswered. One to Brigitte received a swift response: *You're forgiven btw. Black people don't own cats.*

Brigitte was white, and Genevan, but many short-lived relationships with black men from the Caribbean, in particular, had made her an authority on the things black people did and did not do. Maybe this was a running joke at Brigitte's own expense that Mona was supposed to get but didn't. Or maybe it was an (extended) exercise in empathy. Mona wondered: was it Liesel's fault most of her black friends had scattered to the winds? Was it theirs? Or was it her own—*a deliberate and self-destructive isolation*—just like Liesel had said? *You will need your community*, she had said. *Trust me, you will need them.*

Mona had questions: who was *them*? Mummy in Port Antonio? The strangers who'd shown up with the card? Who was Liesel to designate and insist?

There had been some clarification at the time: *Oh, and don't bother leaning too hard on the Euro-heteros. Brigitte and Elke? Those bitches aren't up to the job.*

Liesel always did have a fondness for sentimental hyperbole and warnings that made little sense. Mona left Brigitte on read. George was sitting like a wraith on the sill of the little window. "You're going to have to let me know what you want," Mona said to it. "I won't know otherwise."

The cat turned to face the little window and smashed its skull against the glass.

III.   Mona wandered into the living room and stood there. She'd stripped the walls and shelves of art and trinkets, sold the television, the rocking chair with the creak, the footstool and the gold filigree mirror that had lived above the mantelpiece. The Formica table remained because Mona now hated it, hated it more than cancer, and also it was quite a big thing to ship all the way to Hamburg. The orange bowl had found its way into the living room, though Mona couldn't remember moving it there. The floor was carpeted with a grubby cream short pile, and it seemed a terrible idea to leave a bowl of wet food, the only food George would even look at these days, on that type of surface. She nudged it with her toe, and a tiny cube of meat tumbled from its mound, dragging a brown slick of gravy onto the short pile with it. The living room smelled like overstewed meat and cabbage from the remains of a breakfast Mona had abandoned by the armchair. It grew dark. Mona curled into the armchair and fell asleep.

She called in sick. There was also something wrong with the cat, and with the flat, she explained to her colleague over the phone, the cat and the flat, the flat and the cat, turning a short laugh into a snort over the Seuss-like rhyme. The colleague asked if she was all right and Mona said, "Sure, apart from the cat and the flat, and the flat and the cat," then snorted and hung up. She called in sick again, and then again. She was signed off by a white woman doctor who recommended echinachea and smiling "even when you don't feel like it, even when it hurts." George had failed to eat from the orange bowl for some time and was staring at Mona from the doorway. It had acquired a gold bell on an elasticated red ribbon around its scrawny black neck, the kind of Moulin Rouge bordello choker found on a Lindt Easter Bunny. Mona laughed. "Hussy. What next? Fishnets? Crotchless knickers?" There had been some sort of massacre in the living room; gold Lindt foil littered the carpet, glittering in vicious disco shreds. "No wonder you're not hungry," Mona said. "Isn't chocolate bad for cats?"

The internet said it was. Very bad. George stood in the corner unblinking. A local vet had a free consultation promotion going so Mona rang the number on the flyer that had pushpinned itself to the living room wall. It was so strange to hear the receptionist's voice, like the feeling of being on a listing ship. Mona spoke: "I have a cat that isn't eating, except continental Easter chocolate. And it tried to bash its brains out on the window."

The receptionist said she'd ask the veterinary nurse to call back.

"Nurses?" Mona said. "Veterinary nurses?"

"Yes, a nurse will call you back," the receptionist said.

"I've never heard of that."

"Okay. Well now you have." For some reason, the receptionist sounded personally offended. There was a tense second of silence before the dial tone rang in Mona's ear like a Klaxon. In the kitchen, her laptop was open, and her mother was at the stove in Port Antonio with her back to London as always. "Mummy?" Mona said to the screen. "Mummy, what did you make of Liesel?"

"Your friend who died?"

"Liesel was my girlfriend, Mummy. For years. You know that, so please stop pretending now." Mona gripped her temples. "But nobody lost their life over it. I don't think that's what happened."

Mummy's face appeared up close, her black eyes fracking for misery or sense, Mona couldn't quite tell.

"I don't understand you, Mona. Why you don't come fly home and eat something? How many years since you finish that degree? When you coming home fi see me? You lose weight."

Mona closed the laptop then opened it again. Mummy didn't seem that hot on empathy, which felt like it might be relevant. In the search results a way forward had presented itself. The refresher course was correspondence only and £114.99 from eBay. You received a ring binder in the post, and you had to complete the modules, or so-called "stages," that were separated by brightly colored file dividers. The stages were:

1. Acceptance
2. Adjustment
3. Animals
4. The Human Heart
5. Revision

The seller had offered a sample exercise, taken from the Adjustment stage:

Empathy is like a muscle. It can grow stiff with underuse. This whole course is like a workout for your empathy muscle! So, let's start out with some light stretches. Place your arms above your head and reach up onto your tip toes as high as you can. Hold for a count of three. Then bend from the waist, keeping your legs straight, and try to touch your toes. Repeat x3. While you stretch, ponder the last time you felt understood by someone. What did they do to make you feel that way?

Mona held her arms above her head and felt she'd made a start already. The little window was open, and George was balanced on the sill and ducking, about to launch itself into the patchwork of backyards below. It took a minute to drag the cat back inside. "We're four floors up, George. If you want to go for a stroll we can talk about that." George was soft and deceptively solid in her hands. Its heart was beating steadily. "You're okay, I think," Mona said. "You're all right."

This was what she told the veterinary nurse. "There have been incidents, but I feel things may be all right."

It was late and the veterinary nurse sounded tired. "Well, if you have any more problems, just call us back."

"I will," Mona said. "Good night." She hit Buy Now on the refresher course. Through the little window, now open just a chink, the rich, tangy scent of barbecue snuck into the flat. The breeze that carried it was just warm, the sweet breath of a premature summer.

IV.   "Are you trying to kill yourself?" Mona asked George after she found it with its face fully submerged in its water bowl. "Is that what's happening here?"

The veterinary nurse confirmed this could indeed be the case. "When they're worn out, they sometimes do this. Is George in pain? Can you tell?"

George didn't seem to feel anything. But then Mona wasn't sure if this assumption was merely a reflection of her own inadequacy. "So, what now?" Mona asked.

"Well, if George isn't in pain, there's not much to do."

There was a long pause. Mona could hear her heart beating and that dial tone Klaxon sounding off, faint, somewhere distant.

"But, how can I live like this?" she asked.

"Hmm. That's a tough question," the veterinary nurse said. "I'm afraid I don't know."

"Well, should I bring the cat in?" Mona almost shouted. That Klaxon was intimate; her head was full of blaring noise. The living room, the flat, the whole world was a battering ram of noise. "To see the vet?"

"The vet? The vet?" The veterinary nurse had started acting like she was living in a totally different reality. "What for? I don't know how that would help."

"She might prescribe antidepressants?"

The veterinary nurse laughed. "For a cat?"

Plenty of articles on the internet had talked about psychotropic medications for cats. It wasn't such a woo-woo idea. "I have to do something," Mona said. "George is trying to kill itself. It's going to succeed. I have to do something to stop it, don't I?"

"Like I said," the veterinary nurse groaned. "There's nothing much you can do."

"I was right not to believe in veterinary nurses," Mona said and hung up.

Mrs. Howath had died. The daughter had slipped another note under the door: *If you want to send flowers. I know you two were close. She was very sad about your partner. I'm sorry about that, by the way. And I'm sorry I never said so.*

"Are you grieving?" Mona asked George. It stared back as usual, unblinking.

V. Mona sent flowers. She sent roses dyed an artificial purple ombré—the erstwhile colour of Mrs. Howath's hair. What kind of people send flowers and cards and earnest missives of support? Not people like Mona, typically, which was possibly why she hadn't received any; they had no doubt found their way to Hamburg like everything else. There was some debate over whether sending flowers to Mrs. Howath—or rather sending flowers to Mrs. Howath's absence, or whatever else was left in her place now that she was dead—represented a genuine act of kindness or merely a response to a tacit request. George thought the latter, while Mona remained on the fence. In the bath she asked Liesel about kindness.

"I can't say I did it for Mrs. Howath. Or her daughter. I don't know why I did it."

"Maybe you did it for you," Liesel said.

"So, I'm just selfish?" Mona laughed, and the echo stung. "Is that what you're saying?"

"Maybe. One woman's selfishness is another's self-empathy."

"Self-empathy?"

"I imagine it'll be on your refresher course."

"Oh, so now you're making fun of me? Nice."

"No, I'm not. The course is… a step in the right direction, I think. Anyway, maybe you sent the flowers to be kind to you. That might be okay, given the circumstances."

"Given the circumstances, given the circumstances, blah." Mona yanked the ball chain with her toe and freed the plug. She let the water drain from around her. "I'm sick of that line. You sound like a fucking quack. I don't see how any of this figures."

"It's like taking the cat," Liesel went on. She'd become tediously philosophical, borderline therapeutic, since she left. "You wanted company, so you took the cat."

"George is the worst company." It had tried the drowning trick again, and despite the distinctly un-British heat, which clogged every room of the flat like a gag, Mona kept the little window shut now all the time. "I definitely didn't want the cat," she shouted.

"I stand corrected. Okay, how about this: When you looked in the mirror—which was an antique and you shouldn't have left out in the fucking street by the way—you wanted to see the kind of person who would adopt a dead woman's cat."

"Look where that got me," Mona said and hauled herself out of the dry bath. "For fuck's sake."

"Vanity is merely an expression of deep need, Mona," Liesel called after her through the steam. "Mona? Mona! It's okay to need, you know. Go and see those women from the collective. They're just around the corner and—"

Mona shut the bathroom door and wandered naked into the bedroom. A kerfuffle was taking place in the wardrobe. Rustling and gentle shuddering came from inside it like something from an eighties comedy horror.

"George." Mona had a vague sense of its antics being funny, but perhaps in an alternate universe. In this world, life with it had become a tightrope. "George?"

The cat had found its way onto the rail. In an impressive display of balance and flexibility it had wound its head through a wire coat hanger.

Mona got on the phone. "Is it likely a cat would try to hang itself?"

"No," the veterinary nurse said and sighed. "I don't see how that could happen." George was dangling, languid under Mona's arm. "But is it possible?" she asked, eyeing its scruff for ligature marks.

"Not really." The veterinary nurse wasn't paying attention. People were sing-yelling in the background. It sounded like a party. "I highly doubt it…"

Different noise filled the line then, persistent, like tinnitus. Staring at the flat black crown of George's head, Mona felt a bite of panic. It really was going to succeed, and it couldn't. "I think I should bring it in. Right now."

"We're closed."

"It's two thirty. It's Tuesday."

"Okay, we're not closed. But it's Linda's birthday today. And she's fragile, bless her—her husband cheated, he gave her an STI, not an incurable but anyway—she's had a hard six months. We're celebrating."

"I've had a hard six months. I'VE HAD A FUCKING HARD SIX MONTHS!"

"Have you thought about throwing a party for George? It might cheer him up." The veterinary nurse was drunk out of her mind. Mona hung up the phone.

The refresher course came in a large box with excess packaging and a nonapology for the delay. *Life conspired against me*, a note inside read. *I hope upon completion of this course you will understand. Please note: Correspondence is UNILATERAL.* The seller, who also seemed to double as the course tutor, had opted for fat polystyrene peanuts and reams of brown paper and had bound the ring binder over and over in cling film and bubble wrap. It was tiring just to look at the box. Mona got to work, grudgingly. The whole production was insanely archaeological; it had a stultifying effect on the mind. She plowed on—what else was there? The strangers who came, the headwrap and the skullcap round the corner? Who could say? Maybe they were figments. There was definitely George, though, watching in the half-light from its favorite corner.

"Look what I'm doing," Mona said to it across the room. "I'm sick of myself. You must be sick of me, too."

George yawned.

"Fair," Mona told it.

The ring binder was finally free. Mona leafed through The Human Heart, printed, like the rest of the course, in neat handwriting on A4 lined paper—a scam. One exercise asked you to literally walk around in someone else's shoes: *Borrow some from a friend or neighbor, anyone with different size feet to you. Different taste, too, ideally! At a push, a pair from a charity shop will do.* Another exercise invited the reader to help a homeless person by asking them to lunch. Mona looked up. George had crept closer, a stealth mission to accomplish… what? It sucked a polystyrene peanut up from the ground in one rapid and precise dip.

"What?" Mona didn't hear herself speak. George was barely gagging, allowing the obstruction to bulge and water its eyes. "What the—"

She scrambled, then. Across the short pile, over to George, scrambled for what seemed like an age. Contact was violent. Mona seized its skull and forced its jaw open and pinched around inside, grazing her skin on its sharp, mincing teeth. She wrestled it, and the bout felt monumental, too evenly matched. George turned and squirmed. When a bit of white polystyrene appeared, Mona heard herself yell. "What the fuck is wrong with you? Why do you want to die? Am I not enough? Is that it? Is it so fucking terrible here with me?"

She was ridiculous. Sick of herself and ridiculous and taking it all out on a cat. The regurgitated peanut lay on the short pile between them, slimy and stillborn. They considered it. Mona's hands found her head. She breathed hard behind her palms. George watched her, unblinking.

"Mona?" Mummy's voice dragged Mona into the kitchen. Her round brown face filled up the laptop screen. "Mona? What happen there? Mona? I hear something happen."

"Nothing. The cat." The little thumbnail showed Mona she'd changed. Her own face reminded her of neglected fruit. She exhaled slowly. "It was nothing."

"Nothing? What cat? Sound like the whole world turn upside down over there."

"I think it did, Mummy," Mona said. She closed the laptop. "That was exactly what happened."

In the living room, George was sitting on the discarded ring binder, unblinking. Mona scooped it up and pinned it to her breast, its small, satisfying weight balanced in the crook of her arm. "You're nuts," she said to the familiar crown of its head as they left the flat. "You're totally demented." The strangers from the collective had left an invite taped to the door. *We're having a BBQ, join us! Text us!* along with a number. Mona pocketed it, half thinking she might go. She descended the stairs. She held the cat with one hand and the bannister with the other to steady herself. She was steadied. George was calm and warm, its ears twitching against her collarbone. They walked the ground-floor corridor slowly, under the blinking striplight, passing a jumble of dirty running shoes outside a neighbor's door, the doormat that said Welcome, the stack of abandoned mail for residents long gone that never got much larger, or much smaller, that maybe contained something addressed to Liesel—

Mona pushed into the garish outside. The street was alive and gross— uncomfortably warm and hectic with cars, buses, people. She dodged a girl with shopping bags, a couple holding hands, a suit on his phone. Out the corner of her eye she thought she saw the woman in the black skullcap, slipping away into the crowd. It was possible to chase her, say something about the barbecue, make contact. It seemed possible, outside in the sunlight. But first there was George. She set it down gently on the road between two parked cars. "Liesel would've loved you," she said and rolled her eyes. "Off you go." George didn't look back. Mona watched from her knees on the curb as the heavy traffic rushed past.

THE HEART

VICTORIA CHANG

Someone trimmed the tree.
Maybe there are no answers.
Small bits of blue sky through it.

FIRST OF JUNE

VICTORIA CHANG

Lightning is staged, rain
waits behind the tornado.
The curtain stays closed
until someone falls in love.
Then they move aside for wind.

HIERONYMUS BOSCH BEACH BLANKET BINGO, SUMMER 2020

SYLVIA LEGRIS

The water is fine, a wave of unearthly delight swallowed holus-bolus.

The beach is a game board of umbrella & umbrella, torso & orifice, a vortex of engorgement & vomit & vice versa & back.

"Statecraft," says the bird wearing the plague mask a-perch the lifeguard chair, "is whatever floats your boat."

"C-19!" bellows the host.

"The host is the parasite's parasite…" (Miroslav Holub)

The crowd is a thousand-crackle pyrotechnic with a stroboscopic tail: *Me it's me it's me…*

"Caligula!" yells the host with regal enunciation.

An upsurge against a grisaille sky; a bombette of *Hoax hoax hoax* accompanied by an aerial gold lace effect.

A flourish of hocus-pocus, then, "The water is fine," chirps the bird astride the lifeguard chair.

"Don't you 'I love you' me," says the one impaled on the harp to the one with the knifed hand holding a die.

ON SUNDAY I WATER THE PLANTS

REBECCA WOLFF

Just joking my days are chaotic
the way I like them
these lines are demon-
strative

but a week is a round
number

a week is measured in days and there are seven
just like the fingers on my hands without those ones I

forget, chopped off, bitten off, fell off from scurvy and flesh-
eating: intentionally brutal. Painfully severe. Tens of

thousands of extremes
in the medium

daily.
Every day. Every
single day.

QUAIL IN THE BIBLE

BRIAN BLANCHFIELD

Quail in Numbers come once, second,
in circumstances much the ones
in Exodus. It's in repetition

quail become a form. Or anything
whereof wallpaper's spread, or poetry: the same
orange repeating in one tree
kind of thing. A wilderness of a kind.

A wallpaper of quail in the Bible, then,
to show the episode self-
subsequent, or to alternate the two verses

as splotches of scene: the camp the same
in each, unshaded, stony, chaparral;
in each the murmurs arising as miscreance;
the mixt multitude, and mosaic quail—

in great number, quails
came and *coming up cover'd the land*; on a wind
going out from the Lord likewise

befell the hungry. Thus from
thus the miracle splits. In one, manna follows
the skyfall quail. In the other,
the covenant comes with wrath. Godsend still

in their teeth, the chosen foretold to die
die in Numbers. And quail fluster
filled two cubits of air.

How much was a cubit? What counts
as a murmur? A heel to knee, or knee to hip
distance; a walking complaint
not yet consensus. The quail refrain

can nourish the hunch, the sacrilege
at which even alone a young reader could quail,
whose quiet lap goes numb beneath it:

that this testament is instead a treasury; it
leaves the variant tellings in, so recurrences are
historical by accident. I read the wallpaper
in the room we kept the Bible in;

I slalomed the negative space
between tableaux, improvising a circuit
in the print on Old Providence Road.

It was twenty years before I learned
from a classicist twenty years retired,
in a seminar whose every window framed
the open Sonoran, western quail darting about,

that the life of Jesus, as we have it, is a form
of the life of Socrates. The lecturer, living
lover emeritus of Robert Duncan, took me

after Greek Influence on Early Christianity
to coffee. Everything on the table, the bed
and poem the poet found and put him in;
the shepherd figure Theocritus to Paul;

Pindar to Montessori, the individual soul;
tutelage itself. When quail favor a person
with their passage through, it is ever as if

from nowhere—that much bears out—
to pastor an acre of creosote,
commonly. But covey, not plenty, not plague's
the collective of quail that come.

Reading, last Christmas, the concordance I'd found,
ministering the cholla spline in my heel, I spotted
the flock, some seven the season retained

from hatch or bachelor-patched into family.
About's their preposition; if there are quail
there are quail about. About our airbnb
in Joshua Tree, so named for the yucca

so named by the Mormons who
found in the form, arms raised, a Joshua, who
was a form of Moses, a furtherance,

it dawned on me the meal I'd made the night before
from whatever we had's what the Israelites
are said in Psalms to have bewailed without
since Egypt: fish and melon and cucumber.

It wanted bread, John said. The quail mill
meanwhile the cholla, yucca, the creosote
that overall and so evenly speck an expanse

that rising in flight would reveal it
as the gameboard they run, tile
by Mojave tile, in teams. It's in peace they peck
apart; they wander, quail, dispersing most

when least is anything to heed. In danger, though,
fleet as rabbit scatter, quail reunion
on the move is their mark. They gather, going.

Did desert ancients, extrapolating, ask
under threat that quail spirit obtain? Several
started when I rose, favoring my surer step,
cursing, Christmas, pre-pandemic.

for Norman Austin

THE WHITE HOUSE

GILLIAN CONOLEY

The house was no longer a toy.

It was beginning to take to the horizon.

It was attaining a righteousness.

It was getting into a facelessness.

Someone tried posting a video of it, a blur

under a wolf moon, a verdant expanse,

but was shoved down before pressing send.

We shall have these truths.

Few ever really got to live there.

It was smaller than anyone ever expected.

Its lights were dimmed, though guards remained

in dreamy wigs, roasting pigs, as portraiture

was encouraged in this icebox—

Snow globe, raindrop,

a tiny, naked agent circling the perimeter

as stars appear, disappear in dark skies.

Few acts are intolerable to a house.

Bed mites on night duty.

Riot gear,

a kiln of $x = y$.

A woman looking up under a glass pane.

A man climbing a wall.

We people, who cease to be useful.

Ron Nagle

POCKET MONEY

In the late evenings Olympic Billiards was crowded with young players and hawkeyed boys who watched more games than they played and men who moved between the tables and never played. The pool hall was twice as wide as it was long. It was a bright place, ice blue under the halogen bulbs; the tables were clean, and they played music at low volume and infrequently. Tacked above the unused coat rack was an old framed photo of Bill Clinton that had been there since the place had opened. At the back was a counter with stools. Regulars knew not to sit on the stools, leaving them for the employees of the pool hall. The girls behind the counter were older than most of the regulars and unfriendly. They sold sodas and pretzels and dried squid on a deposit system: you deposited your credit card number and afterward, whenever you wanted, you withdrew snacks and cigarettes. No alcohol was served now, and it hadn't been since a boy had died some months ago in a drunken brawl.

The place had been recommended to me by Man Suk, who knew about all the different joints in Koreatown. Olympic Billiards was owned by wealthy Korean brothers who only hired immigrants. The Persians working valet for the restaurant downstairs, Blue Night Sushi, did double duty as security for the pool hall. "That's something you might do," Man Suk told me after he took me to the pool hall that first night. "Manage the Persians for the boys in the hall." He talked about the job as if it were a done deal, but he never introduced me to anyone and didn't tell me who I could go see to find out about it. Man Suk was a difficult person to be friends with. You couldn't ask him for anything because once he found out you wanted something from him—even if it was something he'd offered to you in the first place—it meant the end of the friendship. He had, however, paid for my yearlong membership to the pool hall. I could come and go whenever I wanted.

I had borrowed enough money from some fellows in Seoul to see me through three lean months, but I was nearing the end of them now. If I couldn't find a job, I would have to go back. Sometimes I thought about finding a woman. If I found a woman, I could marry her for my papers and get a real job, maybe work construction again. No one wanted to hire a Korean without papers, and when I asked Man Suk about it, he said a guy like me would sue if I got hurt on the job.

With or without one I would have to go back anyway, but there was nothing to go back to, and no one was waiting for me at home. The options open to me didn't look good, and it made me feel foul to sit there in my rented room and think about what a low place it was that I occupied in the world, which was a low and foul place to begin with.

I showed up at the pool hall every night, but no one came to me about a job, and I was no friendlier with the employees, who kept to themselves. To Man Suk I said nothing, of course. Sometimes I got hopeful about scrounging up money somewhere, walking into a bit of luck. Around Man Suk I was careful to act as though such things weren't a thought to me at all.

He took me out to a meal every other night or every third night, and afterward we played a bit of pool with fellows he knew. When Man Suk was not at the pool hall, I liked to stand alone with my back to the blacked-out window near the counter and watch the action. I was always thirsty after standing for so long, but I had no credit card to deposit with the unsmiling girls at the counter. Soft drinks have a way of sounding precious and delightful when they're being opened and drunk by other people. After putting in my hours at the pool hall, I went home and sucked the water out of my bathroom faucet.

Eventually things turned friendly with one regular, a short fellow with fat Buddha ears who went by a name I didn't know a Korean could call himself. After I strategically lost some money to him, he asked my age and told me I could call him brother. He was almost forty years old, but his fatness shaved off a good decade. After I paid him, we went out to the balcony to smoke.

"What kind of name is Enoch?" I asked.

"Get you some religion, boy." He kept a half-drained Coke can as his ashtray, and every time he tapped his cigarette, the ash made a nice sound as sizzling meat would make: *sssshhhaa*. "A Koreatown church will give you everything you need: old clothes, furniture, hot meals on Wednesdays, Fridays, and Sundays, women, girls."

"I don't know."

"A lot of women in the church."

"I need money if I want a girl."

Enoch considered this. He pulled up his mouth and shrugged. "This is true."

I looked across the street at another blue-painted joint with blue lanterns hanging over the door. The sushi restaurant downstairs had blue doors and walls too; the pool hall's sign and carpet were the same Egyptian blue. When I pointed this out, Enoch said the only thing he knew was that all the blue joints were owned by the same Koreans.

We went back into the pool hall. I stood back and watched Enoch. He came in every night, but he looked for fast players who played short games because he liked to pay the hourly rates rather than go in for a membership. After a while an employee came over to give Enoch a hard time.

"Yeah, but," Enoch said after the employee had given his spiel.

"Yeah, but? Finish your thought."

Enoch rested his double chin on his cue stick. "No thought at all, brother."

The employee calculated aloud the various ways Enoch might save money by paying for a yearlong membership.

I stopped listening at this point and paid attention instead to the way an older man was watching the employee. When it was clear the employee had lost Enoch's attention completely, the man shook his head a little, and the employee moved away. The game went on, and I watched as the man disappeared behind a yellow door; the employee moved around and around the pool hall; Enoch waved a boy over and ordered a Red Bull. He'd won, but he was also pleased with himself about something that had nothing to do with the game.

"Give me your number," Enoch said suddenly. "We can have gamjatang where my girl cashiers. She's working tomorrow night and we can eat for practically nothing."

I patted my empty pocket. "It's been about two days since I lost it on the bus. Still no sign of it."

He clicked his teeth sympathetically before leaning his head back to pound the last of his Red Bull. His throat was ringed with skin tags where his flesh met the band of his T-shirt. "Come by here tomorrow night. We'll meet up and go over together."

Soon after he left, I stationed myself at the back of the pool hall by the counter. The shift change happened at midnight. The skinny young Koreans who worked the early-evening hours disappeared one by one and older, wilder faces emerged out of the back rooms. An employee the regulars called Guatemala came out of a back room zipping up a black pullover all the way to the top so that only half his beakish face showed. He came over to sit on a stool in front of the countergirls. He watched the action over his shoulder, his body angled at the countergirl called Eun Hae. She looked very young and fresh and everything about her was sweet, even the way her black bra straps slipped out from under her sleeveless chiffon top. After Guatemala moved away she punched some buttons on the credit card machine, and as it spewed out its paper entrails, she looked me over without pretending not to look me over, which interested me.

Guatemala hadn't been away two minutes when he came over to her again. He zipped his pullover up and down and up again, and when he asked her something in English, she readily responded, her tone and mannerisms transforming her into a girl totally foreign to me. I realized I'd mistaken her for a normal Korean girl; that washed away some of the brightness of her gaze, and I decided I'd go home early.

In the morning I found a tortoiseshell cat banging around the trash cans behind the boarding house. It didn't like my presence at all. I stared it down even as it threw everything it had at me, hissing and screeching, swishing a black tail that swelled to twice its size. I sat on a cinderblock and shook a bag of shrimp-flavored crackers at it until it calmed down. We opened the bag together.

"Acting crazy is for crazies," I said. "You're not crazy, are you?" I wagged a cracker at it until it padded over to me. He sniffed it but wouldn't eat out of my hand. Cats have got queer tongues. When they lick you, their tongues feel like the way new tires sound over gravel.

We finished the crackers. The morning was hot, so I made him a lean-to out of a ramen box. As I enticed him to take shade inside, I thought about going to see Man Suk later. I'd spent the last of my money to keep my room at the boarding house. I needed the pool hall job but asking Man Suk for it directly was out of the question. Sometime in the middle of my thinking and dozing, a homeless woman in a ratty college sweatshirt appeared silently. Despite her quiet ways she scared away the cat. That annoyed me right from the start. She paid me no attention as she rooted through the trash cans that belonged to the boarding house. I pretended to be drunk and pulled my baseball cap low over my face. When I leaned back against the wall, I could spy on her through the sun-bright gap between the bill of my cap and my nose. She worked fast. In no time at all she'd pulled out cans and glass jars and old light bulbs. She stuffed these into an old duffel bag slung over her thick shoulders. It rattled and sang as she zipped it up.

When she moved away, I got up and followed her from a distance. She walked down Olympic Boulevard, digging through the occasional bin but never staying very long at any one place. It seemed she had her favorites. Only at these special bins did she let herself linger, examining items of refuse as though each held extraordinary value and only the size of her duffel bag was keeping her from taking them all. She extracted hundreds of cans and other recyclables in the hours I followed her, but she disturbed nothing and left no signs of her foraging. In silence she stamped cans down to nothing and emptied bottles of their liquids before stashing them in her duffel bag. At one point she found a children's picture book and this she looked over carefully before tucking it into the band of her sweatpants. She was small and dark and thick everywhere, except in her hands, and she worked quickly, so quickly we reached the recycling center before noon.

Just before she went in, she turned and glanced behind her as if she knew of my presence. I ducked into a Korean-owned auto body shop across the way. Inside I asked the Hispanics for the owner who came out wiping his hands on a rag.

"What kind of trouble is it?" said the owner.

"It's my piece-of-shit Kia. Whenever I start the car, the tire light keeps coming on. I've checked everything out myself. There's nothing wrong with the tires. I don't know why the light should keep coming on like that."

The owner nodded. "That's no trouble at all. You put the key in the ignition but don't start the engine. When the tire light comes on, press down on the brake a couple times, slowly. Start the engine on P and tap the brakes. Light should turn off."

I thanked the owner and asked him what I owed.

"Nothing. Have you parked the car out front? I can do it for you now, if you'd like."

"No, that won't be necessary. I walked over from work." I mimed digging, patting down my empty pockets as if I were looking for my wallet but the owner lightly shoved me out the door.

"Come back and see us when you've got real trouble," he said.

I walked out into the noon sun and baked under it as if I were waiting for the pedestrian light to turn green. At the recycling center the homeless woman was loitering out front, talking to another bum and sharing a cigarette. They smoked it down to nothing and she finally moved away. Her duffel bag had deflated to an eel across her back.

She moved back up Olympic, swinging her empty Trader Joe's tote bag as she walked. She stopped by a liquor store and came out with an AriZona Big Can. We moved onto Western and stopped in front of a Bank of America ATM where she stamped the empty AriZona can down into a pastel-green UFO. She took a rest in an alleyway that was empty of everything and everyone, even pigeons, and there I showed myself and shoved her down onto the ground.

She looked past me as I did it, her eyes wet. There were age spots on her brown toad's face, a patch of black whiskers across her upper lip. It repelled me to do it, but I dug inside the waistband of her pants to check if she'd stashed her money there. She had, tucked under the children's book. Those damp bills had been clinging to the dead wires of her wild bush like bits of tissue and sanitary pads and love notes as you might find in a shrub near a high school of ill repute, and there was I, plucking the lot of it. I kicked her over onto her side so she wouldn't look at me as I ran out of the alley. Once I was back on the street, I looked for a plastic garbage bag and with it I wrapped my bundle of cash. It was mostly wet fives, the old kind of bill bearing a face carved entirely of blue-martian peaks and valleys, those belonging to that assassinated president, the one so fond of tall hats such as our old yangban used to wear.

There was a men's bathhouse near the pool hall where a fellow could wash and rest for eight dollars if he showed up before four o'clock. Most days eight dollars was too much money for a bath, but today had been a good day, and I didn't want to spoil it by waiting in line behind four other fellows for the single stall back at the boarding house.

I went in and bought myself a token and washed myself and scrubbed each of my paper bills with a bar of the cucumber-scented soap the sauna gave out for free, and afterward we dried ourselves on the heated floors of the large, open sleeping room. I bought a hard-boiled egg for a dollar and some rice punch that had been chilled in such a deep part of the cooler it'd nearly frozen into slush. Warm and filled with food, I dozed for a while then went out into the evening. It was early yet and cool; the sky was violet. I moved down Sixth toward the pool hall with twenty-three dollars left in my pocket, which was a hard truth to accept.

I met up with Enoch and together we walked over to the restaurant where his girl cashiered. We shared a large pot of gamjatang and Enoch's girl charged us only for our bottle of soju, which impressed me because it seemed to me she wielded a lot of power for a waitress, and one so small and ugly. I took out some of my cash to leave her a nice tip, which pleased Enoch greatly, I could tell. We walked back to the pool hall with our arms around each other's shoulders and I thought, Now here's the end, here's where I get off.

But surrounded by fellows having a good time in a bright room with a good-looking girl watching the action behind her counter, you don't get to thinking about getting off the ride just yet, so I joined a game with Enoch and two fellows. That's what I was doing when Man Suk came and told me about a job. I had all my money riding on that game, but when he told me to follow him downstairs, I handed my cue stick to a kid who'd been spectating and went out of the pool hall.

Down in the parking lot the Persians were playing hacky sack. Man Suk spoke to them in what sounded like Spanish. They spoke back in sullen tones, and the hacky sack disappeared into someone's pocket. I realized it was Man Suk himself who managed the Persians for the owners of the pool hall.

He walked past Blue Night Sushi, and we crossed the street, right to the blue-painted joint I'd pointed out to Enoch. There was a little sign posted to the left of the door with the English words *Salt Water* carved into dark stone.

"It's a noraebang," said Man Suk. "They'll pay cash, and you can take home your share of the tips. Grand opening is next week."

When we went inside, the few employees there greeted Man Suk deferentially but informally at the same time. Two wispy youths with similar dry-haired shag cuts came out from behind the counter, where they'd been stacking soju glasses into a pyramid, and poked gentle fun at him for something he'd said last week to a man they referred to as the manager of the place. I was relieved to learn that I wouldn't have to work under Man Suk. The fact of his getting me a job as he'd promised elevated him substantially in my mind, but it seemed to me he was one of those fellows who lives exactingly by the rules known only to his own mind and looks down on everyone else for failing to intuit them.

"This is the joker I was telling you about," he said to the employees, clasping my shoulder. "Go show him around." He took a seat at the bar and called over a handyman who'd been testing out the POS on the hostess stand. We left them as they got into a conversation about the poor sound quality of the speakers installed in Blue Night Sushi.

There was nothing much to see in the main room which was partitioned into a sort of receiving area which included the bar and hostess stand and a waiting room behind a screen where you could sit with three or four others and watch pop music videos on a curved television. I followed the employees out of this main room and down a hall which had been painted gunmetal black and was mirrored on the ceiling. There was another bar in the center of the room, twice as large as the one in the front, and standing behind that was another employee who paid us no mind as he marked up an MCAT prep book.

"You work at the pool hall?" said one of the employees, the only kid with an American name on his badge. If it was to be believed, he was called Joey.

I said I'd been coming and going there for a while.

"We made a poor show of it in the soft open last week," said the other employee, who had bad skin and a bashful smile. He was called Tae Won. He asked me to please call him Teddy. This, despite his name badge identifying him as T.W.

"No one knows what the fuck they're doing here," said the one called Joey.

"How many of you are there altogether?" I asked.

"Six guys, seven now that you're here. Boss doesn't like part-timers. You'll have to show up every night if you want to work for him."

I said that that would be fine.

At something in my expression, Joey told Teddy to tell me what the hell it was I was supposed to be doing here. Joey seemed to find the idea of my training, or the training itself, funny.

Teddy went to the bar and got us cans of Sprite. It was warm but fine, the first soft drink I'd had in weeks. "Mostly you'll have to figure shit out for the customers when the songs won't play or they play out of order or the mics don't work."

"And kick out drunks and put them into taxis," Joey said. "Put SpeedTown into your phone. Here's their business card. We only use SpeedTown."

"You want to sell bottles and shots," said Teddy. "But with cheapos you've got to let them think they can just order beer and stay on beer. You watch them. Soon you'll be able to figure out if loading them up on free snacks will sell them on moving on to shots and bottles or if they'll just stick with the beer. Fruit platters come with shots and men won't order those unless a hostess comes in."

"There are hostesses here?" I asked.

"You new to noraebangs or something?" said Joey.

"Just to this one."

"Well, what do you think this place is?"

Teddy let out a yawn. He was missing several teeth, although he could afford very nice shoes. "Aw, leave him alone. You'll pick it up," he said to me. "Just get acquainted with the machine and the programming and the remote. There are manuals in the manager's office."

They went off to look for snacks in the kitchen, and I looked around the place. I went into the VIP rooms, which were large and smelled of carpet shampoo, then slipped into one of the regular rooms. Regular rooms were less private; their doors were glass. I turned on one of the machines and sat back on the low sofas and cawed into the microphone. My voice shot up and cracked down the walls.

Man Suk opened the door and popped his head in. "Come see about a uniform."

I took a medium-size black shirt and black pants and Man Suk told me to get my hair cut more stylishly. He looked at my shoes. "Throw those away," he said. Then he took me and Joey and Teddy to see the fellow who managed the place.

The manager was called Ko. Ko said and did nothing as Man Suk spoke at length about the importance of loyal employees. I watched Ko as he rubbed his lean, handsome face with the backs of his dark hands. He had large black eyes, which were shadowed, and thin lips and his black hair was combed back from a high, brown forehead.

"This is the kid I was telling you about," Man Suk said, finally, after he'd run out of steam. He took a seat on a couple of cases of toilet paper.

Ko stopped rubbing his face and didn't look quite at me as he introduced himself pleasantly enough and in a lightly self-deprecating way which made everyone laugh.

I stepped forward, and we shook hands.

"Can you start next week?" he asked.

"I can start now."

That made Joey and Teddy laugh.

"Good, good," Ko said. "Come by when you can and learn the ropes. Hours are five till two, every night. We open on holidays. That okay with you?"

"That's okay with me."

"Man Suk told you about the hair?"

Joey and Teddy touched their heads, but I didn't. They looked at each other. Teddy shrugged his shoulders. It was Joey who finally spoke up. "Hyung, I know you've told us before, but I can't pay for a haircut at Atelier until I get my first paycheck."

I looked at Man Suk, who looked unbothered by the conversation. He sat picking at his teeth with the corner of a business card. "Atelier girls are good," he said.

"Everyone goes to Atelier," Joey said.

Ko said nothing.

We trooped out of his office. I wanted a glimpse of the hostess girls, but I saw only electricians and the same studious fellow behind the counter. Ko took his place and passed around shots of what he called the house special, a salty, snappy little thing that flamed down my throat and slimed my tongue with something that tasted of the white stuff in pomelos. Ko then gave each of us three hundred-dollar bills and said we should buy good shoes and good haircuts and not to show up at work ever looking less well-off than our customers. "Never let anyone feel guilty about spending money here," he said. "If the employees of a joint look good and healthy and careful, then customers feel it's a good place to go. They won't question their coming. They want to have a nice place to go. They'll come back if they think you're nice too."

After that I took a bus home but the walk back to the boarding house took me hours. I got off at the wrong stop because the way the Americans say *Sepulveda* and *San Vincente* sounds nothing at all like the way I see those letters in my mind, and it was like waking from a dream when the bus shot past the right stop, and the right way to call those streets coiled out of those speakers. But I didn't mind the walk. My pockets held more money than I'd had in weeks. I smoked two cigarettes and I smoked them freely, knowing I could now make enough money for all the packs I wanted.

In my room I found an old hanger that the previous boarder had left behind, and I hung up my new uniform. I lay on my mattress and admired the way it swayed this way then that in the breeze that came in through the open window. It was a body hanging from a rod, or kelp in dark water—that depended on how you saw things, and who you were.

HARVESTERS

Alfonso stood before the cracked mirror on their bedroom wall and considered putting on a jacket and a tie. It was a cool morning, but by afternoon, heat and humidity would be clutching at his neck. Before her reign of silence began, Inimfon had said one last thing about the new church: if you stepped inside the building without a jacket, she'd heard, you could catch a fever from the power of the ACs.

When Come Ye Ministries first opened its doors on Igoke Street, just a short walk from Alfonso's own church, Inimfon would, every few days, bring to his ears some searing detail about the pastor or the services and watch his face, waiting for a reaction.

"I heard they share jollof rice to their members every Sunday. Can you imagine?"

"Alfonso, they now have two Sunday services at that church. Soon they'll start putting canopies in the street for the overflow!"

It was from Inimfon's lips that Alfonso learned that the pastor of Come Ye Ministries was nicknamed Daddy Too Much, because he had countless SUVs and an American wife. "They say the first time the pastor and his wife met, she fell flat on her face; she couldn't even stand to shake his hand because of the power of his anointing." After glancing at Alfonso's stony face, she added, "People will believe anything. Can you imagine?"

This morning, they were both quiet as they prepared for church, their separate routines well established. Alfonso buttoned up his shirt and tucked it into slightly oversized pants that he held up with a peeling belt. With Inimfon in tow, Alfonso marched out to his old car, holding his King James Bible and sermon notes—today he'd be preaching Part III of his Unlocking Divine Abundance series. They settled in, and Alfonso turned on the engine, causing the car to spasm like a dying beast. Inimfon did not wince at the engine's angry rattling like she often did, nor did she dab at the sweat forming above her upper lip or fan her neck with an old church flyer. She did not lean forward to fiddle with the air conditioner, which hadn't worked in years.

It was about six months ago when Inimfon had mentioned the ACs at the new church. She'd been helping Alfonso set up for Sunday service in the assembly hall of the primary school in Obalende where his church met. Standing with arms akimbo, she'd glared up at the lazy ceiling fans that spread warm, dusty air. She stood in that pose for a long time, and when she finally spoke her voice sounded like it was coming from another room. Alfonso said nothing, and after an eternity of stillness his wife sighed. Alfonso heard that sigh as a eulogy for dead dreams, and the weight of his failures came and sat on his shoulders like a yoke. That same day, during the service, Alfonso found himself announcing the start of a fundraising campaign. The church would acquire their own worship space. He called the campaign Build Him a House.

Because the campaign had been divinely inspired, and certainly had nothing to do with the new church a few streets away, Alfonso decided that the forty-two members of his congregation, none of whom were particularly well-off, would somehow be able to raise the millions they'd need to buy land in the Lekki area, where their church was destined to stand. God would work out the details in His mysterious ways. Alfonso began tailoring all of his sermons toward the same message—the negative consequences of a tight fist ("If your hand is closed, how can God put anything into it?"), and the blessings that came from giving, and giving generously, to God and His causes. "And what greater cause can there be than to…" and Alfonso would bellow "Say it with me!" and the church would say it with him—albeit with less and less enthusiasm each passing Sunday—"Build Him a House!" He also began sending his members multiple text messages a week, with Bible quotes and reminders about God's love for cheerful givers.

Alfonso pretended not to notice his membership numbers slowly dwindling, refused to dwell on the empty spaces opening up where bodies used to warm the benches. Each time Inimfon presented him with the numbers after a service, he would say the same thing he always said: "Glory be to God." Last Sunday, after his usual response, she'd asked, quite loudly, "Glory be to God for only seven people?" She didn't wait for an answer, and as she turned away, her words burrowed under his skin.

It didn't help that his calls and texts to his members who had been absent for many Sundays remained unanswered. Brother Ifeanyi had given some excuse about needing to prepare for an exam at school. The young man had remained consistent with attendance for over a year, and Alfonso considered him a protégé of sorts and sometimes asked his opinion on sermons he was preparing, not because Alfonso needed guidance from a novice, but to make Brother Ifeanyi feel included.

Alfonso eased his car out of its parking spot between the cinderblock fence of the compound and his neighbor's Toyota. As he drove onto the street, his mouth was dry and his stomach cramped up. The last time he'd had only seven people at a Sunday service, he'd been a nervous young man preaching out of a roadside shed in Iyana Ipaja. It occurred to Alfonso that Inimfon's stories about the new church might have been her way of seeking communion, of voicing the shared fears lurking in the corners of their minds. He thought about reaching across to take her hand. He knew what it would feel like now: rough and calloused from carrying them both, unlike when they were newlyweds, the light of his dreams burning bright in their eyes.

He had married Inimfon eight years ago for her faith in him, for how readily she'd gone to the places he had envisioned. Before they were married, she would sit in his congregation, week after week, and when he shared his prophecies for the future of his ministry, her *hallelujahs* were the loudest. He'd had no choice but to notice her. Her enthusiasm, the intensity of her gaze on him as he preached, bestowed upon her an alluring quality. Many Sundays, she would stay behind after service to chat, and with time she began to materialize right there with him when he saw himself leading the megachurch of his future. He saw her standing tall beside him in low heels and the old brown hat she wore every Sunday.

What happened instead was that Inimfon, after she'd moved into his one-room face-me-I-face-you in Mushin and bemoaned the single backyard kitchen and fought nine other tenants over the shared bathrooms, decided that Alfonso's income from the church would not sustain them, and neither would the heavenly manna that he prophesied would rain down on them at any moment. When she suggested that Alfonso get a job, he pointed out that he already had one, that harvesting the souls of men was full-time work—one could not serve God and mammon, didn't she know? Of course, Alfonso knew that some preachers had businesses or jobs, but he suspected that this, taking one's eye off the work of ministry, was a slow but sure path to corruption. Besides, he had no head for business, and his only qualification was his calling, which he'd dropped out of

LAUTECH to answer—a decision he tried never to dwell on. He quoted scriptures to Inimfon about ravens bringing food to Elijah, gave her sermons on supernatural provision. In the meantime, he said, they could make do with eating two small meals a day; the hunger might do their souls some good, sharpen their faith.

But Inimfon's faith did not hold. She took a loan from her sister and paid for a shed near Mushin Market, where she cooked and sold food to hungry traders and commuters. When they were not at church, Inimfon was at her shed, chopping and pounding and frying. Whenever he offered help like a good husband, she turned him down. "Save your strength for the church," she'd say with a voice that betrayed nothing.

Soon after Inimfon began her food business, Alfonso, desperate to match her achievement, made a list of ten of the biggest churches in Lagos. He would present these churches with the opportunity to have him guest preach a sermon. It didn't even have to be during a Sunday service, a weekday one would do. Once those megachurch pastors heard his preaching—he had recorded one of his best sermons and made it into a CD—they would be falling over themselves to host him in their air-conditioned sanctuaries. Preaching at a big church would put his name in people's mouths. They would come to his service at Little Lights Primary School, Obalende, to seek him out, the old wooden benches, the heat, the mildew spots on the ceiling all hearkening back to a time when preachers of the gospel didn't need the embellishments of cushioned chairs, multimillion naira audiovisual equipment and one-hundred-member choirs in matching robes.

Alfonso found that the road to a megachurch pastor's office was narrower than the road to heaven. He was met by assistants with identical crisp suits and touchscreen tablets, who politely informed him of their bosses' impossible schedules. In a few churches, he managed to secure hurried meetings with junior pastors who educated him about their ministries' structures and hierarchies and asked stupid questions like, "What Bible school did you attend?" and "Who have you served under?" He crossed his legs and told each of them how he received his calling: at a ministry event when he was a university student, the guest preacher had singled him out from the crowd, waved him to the altar, and prophesied that he, Alfonso, would become a great harvester for the kingdom of God. Alfonso watched the pastors' eyes glaze over. They thanked him for his interest and handed him pamphlets about their School of Ministry,

Discipleship Training, whatever they called it. Where was their fancy school of ministry when he was dropping out of LAUTECH to win souls from the streets of Ogbomoso and all the way to Lagos? Where was their discipleship training when he was preaching in taxis and danfos and molues, getting cursed at by weary commuters with voices raspy from stress and exhaust smoke?

Inimfon had just hired her second server at the eatery when Alfonso first heard the radio advertisement for the Next Level Ministers' Fellowship. Alfonso didn't recognize any of the names on the lineup of speakers, but that was okay, better even—these were the people doing God's work without making noise, without trying to appropriate any of the glory for themselves. The registration fee, inclusive of feeding, conference materials, and four nights' accommodation in Akure, was expensive, yes, but the service of God demanded sacrifice. Didn't Inimfon want him to fulfil his calling? She gave him the money, and he called her First Lady in the Making, promising that when they broke ground on their church building he would remind her of this moment.

Instead, Alfonso returned early from the fellowship emptied and hollowed out, with a bitter taste in his mouth that would remain for years. The "fellowship" was more like a trade fair, with ministers hawking their books, recorded sermons, and anointed olive oil and holy water. All the talk sessions and grass-to-grace testimonies ended with a call to action, to buy something or join something. He'd been expecting a prayer revival, a place where he would be buoyed by a fresh anointing, a new revelation from the Word. Still, Alfonso stayed, hoping to find something that would make the experience, and Inimfon's investment, worth it. On the third day, a sweaty fellow in a velvet suit sidled up to Alfonso and handed him a card with a name, phone number, and the title Solutions Supplier printed in purple ink. When Alfonso asked what exactly he supplied, the man leaned in and whispered, his hot breath fanning Alfonso's neck, "My brother, any healing you want to happen in your church, I can arrange it for you. Blindness, deafness, cripple, craze, even HIV, mò lè hook up." Alfonso left the fellowship that day and avoided Inimfon's questions when he got home. He told himself there had to be a right way to achieve megachurch status, a godly way, without salesmen and arrangers of miracles. He would pray and fast and wait; Alfonso had a calling, and God would do it in His time.

While Alfonso waited, Inimfon acquired more staff and expanded her eatery, upgrading from sand floors to concrete, and from no walls to plywood boards. She replaced squeaky wooden benches with plastic chairs and tables and bought standing fans to cool her customers while they ate. She had less and less energy for his waning prophecies about their future. Her *amens* and *hallelujahs* grew weak like old dishwater. And when she prayed, she no longer spent many minutes calling God by all of His names; she deployed her prayers like arrows at a target, as though she expected God to understand she could no longer afford to spend too much time on her knees. Sometimes, Alfonso grew angry, on God's behalf, and was tempted to point out that everything she had achieved had come from God and not her own effort or wisdom. But whenever he opened his mouth to rebuke Inimfon, a twinge of doubt would cause him to pause and look around him at the one-bedroom apartment they'd moved into, with its own kitchen and bathroom inside the apartment, paid for by Inimfon's sweat, and shame would spread in his chest, taking up so much space that there was little room for breath.

Sometimes, in the early hours of morning when his sleep was interrupted by an inchoate unease, Alfonso discerned that the reason Inimfon adhered to her strict regimen of daily contraceptives even as their sex life withered was not, as she claimed, because they couldn't afford to care for a child, but because Inimfon was wary of the fleshly bond that a child would represent, the added difficulty of extricating herself from him. But he'd never challenged her on this, afraid to have his suspicions confirmed; the closest he'd come was making a joke once about how they should have children so they could increase the numbers at his church. Inimfon hadn't even cracked a smile.

Alfonso slowed the car and took the exit for Obalende; in a few minutes they would arrive at his church. He tried to remind himself that money and numbers were not the most important things for a minister. He took pride in knowing all the members of his church as individuals, knowing what kept their heads from resting easy at night. He was at his best, his most unimpeachable, when he went on his knees on behalf of his small flock, whether it was to ask God to ease the trouble in the Okories' tumultuous marriage, or to pray for healing for Sister Remi, who had sickle cell anemia, or to give thanks with young Faaji, who disappeared every once in a while for weeks on end and resurfaced with a large offering and vague testimonies about God prospering his work. Alfonso was particularly protective of Brother Ifeanyi, with his rough edges and overexposure to Ajegunle's hard streets. It had taken some time but

Alfonso, with God's help, of course, had slowly tamed Brother Ifeanyi. He no longer turned up in church proudly hungover and showing off the bumps and bruises from his latest fistfight, or spent what little money he had gambling on NairaLuck, or wore his ripped jeans so low they exposed the swell and split of his buttocks. Alfonso was proud of his work. The first time he met Brother Ifeanyi, the young man had been caught stealing a mobile phone from an electronics store where Alfonso had gone to hand out his church flyers. The shop owner was holding on to Brother Ifeanyi's shirt collar with one hand, the other brandishing her phone as she threatened to call the police and have him locked up for life. Only Alfonso's pleas, delivered on his knees along with Brother Ifeanyi's, and his promise to personally see to the young man's rehabilitation, had convinced the shop owner to let Brother Ifeanyi go. From that day, Alfonso had taken responsibility for Brother Ifeanyi, making sure he stopped skipping his lectures at Yaba Tech, and that he cut all ties with the girl with whom he'd been fornicating, the same girl he'd been trying to please with the phone he'd been caught stealing.

But now, Alfonso worried that his work might be coming undone, given Brother Ifeanyi's long absence. Without Alfonso's influence, it would be too easy for the young man to slide back into his self-destructive ways.

"Brother Ifeanyi hasn't been answering my calls," Alfonso said to Inimfon, without taking his eyes off the road.

She shrugged. "People are busy these days."

"Too busy to come to church or send a text message?" Alfonso said. "No, no, he needs to do better. If he's absent again today, I'll go and visit him after service."

"Okay."

———

Alfonso parked in front of the two-story building that housed Little Lights Primary School. When he'd approached the headmaster about using the school's assembly hall for his church services, it was only a temporary arrangement. Now, a decade later, Alfonso walked to the school gates with heavy feet, Inimfon's shadow falling across him and partially shielding him from the sun. The school building, with its ash-gray walls grimy from children's fingers, and windows hanging askew from their frames, had become too familiar. Even with his eyes closed, he'd know how to avoid the broken bits of concrete ground within the compound that collected rainwater, how to position himself behind the lectern, to hold it just so because too much weight would cause it to lean to the right.

Alfonso pushed open the gate and knocked on the wall of the plywood shack beside it. The door creaked open and a hand held out the key to the assembly hall, the school's gateman not needing visual confirmation of Alfonso's presence after the loud rattling of his car's engine. They walked to the assembly hall, Alfonso wondering if Inimfon felt the same weight that he did pushing down on him, causing his legs to slow like he was wading through wet sand. He stopped outside the hall, key in hand, but made no move to open the door. He could hear the unasked question forming on Inimfon's lips. He thrust the key at her.

"Start setting up. I'm coming."

She took the key with a puzzled frown. "Where are you going?"

Alfonso hurried out through the school gate, fleeing his wife's gaze.

———

Alfonso turned left at the end of Ferguson Road. The streets were peaceful, as they tended to be this early on a Sunday morning. It had rained in the night, but the air was slowly losing its coolness as the sun rose higher, bathing tired old buildings in a surreal light. Alfonso could almost ignore the FanYogo and Gala wrappers and the Power Horse cans that littered the street and clogged the roadside gutters. The abandoned vehicles on the side of the road, long ago stripped of their doors and fixtures, their vacant spaces staring out like soulless eyes, faded into soft colors on the edge of his vision.

It felt like ages ago when he'd first come across the demolition on Igoke Street. With his car at the mechanic's, he'd taken a danfo that carried him past the site. When he noticed the empty skyline where a cluster of old apartment buildings used to stand, he'd played a guessing game with himself, wondering what would be erected once the rubble was cleared away. It had left him with a strange melancholia; a feeling that, like these buildings, his entire being could be wrecking-balled out of existence with a single stroke. He'd known the day would come when whatever structure had arisen in place of the fallen would feel like it had always stood there, everything so utterly replaceable.

Alfonso hesitated as he approached Igoke Street. He thought about turning around, retracing his steps back to Ferguson and the safety of Little Lights. But there was something more menacing about the spectre of the unseen.

As Alfonso neared the former demolition site, he could make out a white dome-shaped structure, and the closer he got the larger it loomed. Beside the dome stood a billboard with the smiling faces of Apostle Goodwill O. Ofobrukueta (aka Daddy Too Much), and First Lady Lois Ofobrukueta, her lips a slash of red, gold jewelry dangling from her ears, and blond hair framing a pale face. Alfonso had been prepared for this Daddy Too Much to have Jheri-curled hair down to his shoulders, and a shiny robe—a ridiculous picture to go with his nickname. But this was a face stellar in its ordinariness, with a neatly trimmed beard and a low haircut. The apostle was dressed in a white suit that matched his wife's. Alfonso forced his feet to carry him forward, toward the dome, until he was standing before a high white wall with the words Come Ye Global Ministries embossed onto it in gold letters.

Alfonso swallowed past the dryness in his mouth and headed for the gates. He pushed on the pedestrian entrance, not truly believing that such an imposing thing would succumb to his touch. The gate swung open silently to reveal ground paved with interlocking concrete tiles in gray and maroon. The dome turned out to be an enormous freestanding marquee reinforced with glass and steel. At the top of the marquee's entrance, the eyes of Daddy Too Much and his wife gazed down from a large banner, both of them wearing bright smiles, the words Welcome Home printed across their torsos in triumphant font.

Voices seemed to be coming from inside the marquee. This early, the only people in church would be workers helping to set up, and perhaps some of the church's leaders. Alfonso followed the voices.

As soon as he stepped inside the dome, goose pimples studded his skin and he rubbed his arms through the fabric of his shirt to warm them. Against the walls, large floor-standing air conditioners spewed clouds of freezing air. Elaborate chandeliers made of glass and gold and crystal, and swathes of silky fabric, hung from the ceiling, shielding from the eye what he imagined would be the bars and bolts that held up the roof. The room was divided in half by a red carpet that ran all the way to an altar, where tall vases stood bursting with flowers. The altar also featured a shiny pulpit made of polished glass and, behind it, a row of overstuffed armchairs in red and gold upholstery. And once again, a large banner hung behind the altar, displaying yet another photo of the Apostle and his First Lady in matching outfits.

The room bustled with activity—a small group of people held hands, bouncing on their feet and shouting prayers up toward heaven. Others were covering the chairs for the congregation with protective fabric. Young women in high heels, blazers that looked sharp enough to cut glass, and long hair extensions that swayed with their every step floated between the rows placing bulletins and offering envelopes on the seats. Alfonso shook his head. Of course, these were the kinds of people who would be drawn to a church like this: sharp dressers, attractive to the eye but empty on the inside. All shine, no substance.

Alfonso felt a hand on his arm. He looked up at the face of its owner, and his mouth fell open. Brother Ifeanyi glanced around the room before guiding Alfonso toward the exit. Outside the marquee, Brother Ifeanyi avoided Alfonso's eyes. Alfonso assessed the man before him, top to bottom. He looked like an entirely new person in shiny black shoes, dress pants, and a navy-blue blazer.

Alfonso's eye was drawn to the tag hanging from a lanyard around Brother Ifeanyi's neck: Usher.

"Usher? When did you start coming here?" Alfonso asked.

Before Brother Ifeanyi could respond, the swinging pedestrian gate caught their attention and a woman walked in. As she passed them, Alfonso locked eyes with her for a second before she looked away.

"Sister Boma!" Alfonso called out. Sister Boma quickened her steps and disappeared into the freezing marquee. Alfonso spun back to Brother Ifeanyi. "How many of you are here?"

"Just me and Sister Boma," Brother Ifeanyi said, still not looking at Alfonso.

Alfonso didn't know whether to believe him—he could be lying to end the conversation quickly, to get him to leave. But that wasn't about to happen. Brother Ifeanyi, more than any other member of his church, owed him an explanation.

"I can understand if the others just leave like that. But you, too, ehn Ifeanyi?"

Brother Ifeanyi shifted his gaze to a spot on Alfonso's right shoulder. "Pastor Al, I'm finishing school next year, and things are hard. Is there anybody in that your church that has connections, that can give me a good job after I graduate?"

"Have you forgotten that if not for me, you'd be graduating inside prison?"

Alfonso regretted the words as soon as he said them. Still, the image of

Brother Ifeanyi on the day they first met, the boy in torn jeans and a ragged T-shirt, on his knees begging to be rescued, was sharp in his memory. Never mind the sleek clothes he was now wearing, a pathetic future had awaited the boy before Alfonso's intervention. It was Alfonso who deserved an apology.

Brother Ifeanyi broke the silence. "I can never forget how you helped me. But, Pastor Al, I need something different now."

"Yes, you need connections, right?" Alfonso sneered. "You need fraudsters like your Daddy Too Much who sell miracles and blessings, and suck people dry. But I don't blame them; I blame their followers, people like you. All you people care about is money and glory."

Brother Ifeanyi's mirthless laughter caught Alfonso by surprise. "What about you? Every single Sunday with your Build Me a House."

"It's Build Him a House!"

"Whatever," Brother Ifeanyi said. His dismissive tone grated on Alfonso, caused his face to burn with anger. "But since everybody is building houses, who should I listen to? You, or the man of God that built this place and filled it up, times two, in less than a year?"

"That's what you have to say to me?" Alfonso said, his voice rising. "After I treated you like a son, after everything I—"

Brother Ifeanyi looked around him, like he was embarrassed to be anywhere near Alfonso. "Pastor Al, please, I have work to do. Our first service is starting soon."

Brother Ifeanyi hurried away, and Alfonso thought about running after him, ripping that lanyard from his neck, stuffing it down his throat. But the protective heat of his anger was already fading, leaving him colder than when he'd walked into the dome. He reached for his collar and undid the top button, but the tightness in his throat persisted. He felt foolish, standing there by himself like an abandoned lover, and so he forced his feet to move toward the gate.

Outside the church compound, Alfonso's eyes drifted upward to the billboard with the Apostle and his First Lady. He imagined Daddy Too Much preaching a powerful sermon to Alfonso's own congregation, against being unequally yoked with failure: "Your God is not poor, so why should your pastor be? How can you be guided to prosperity by a failure?" He saw his members' eyes narrowing in concentration, heads nodding along, mouths amening in holy agreement. He saw Inimfon in that congregation, freshly enlightened, in a new church hat with ornate feathers that reached for the heavens.

———

Inimfon was wiping the lectern with a rag. She spared Alfonso only a glance as he appeared in the doorway, but how he must look to her, the entire opposite of the things he'd sold her.

On his walk back to Little Lights he'd mulled over Brother Ifeanyi's words. "Build Me a House," Brother Ifeanyi had said. A mistake, or a pointed accusation? He'd become unrecognizable to himself. Maybe the visiting preacher's prophecy all those years ago was a lie, mere theatrics. Or maybe Alfonso would indeed do great things, but they would not be projected from massive screens strategically positioned in a chilly church building the size of a football stadium. Maybe he was made to fellowship with a small community where he knew the people by name and could nurture their individual gifts, where they weren't a massive faceless crowd. Could he win back his runaway congregation? And Inimfon. If he put a new vision on the table, would she stay?

Alfonso took another step into the assembly hall, towards Inimfon. He didn't know how to form the words he knew he should say to her, and so he tried to form his body, the entirety of his being, into a penance—for the smell of dust in the air, the thick cobwebs hanging high up in the ceiling, the terrazzo floor whose shine had long died, for Inimfon's secondhand gray skirt suit and the battered hat she'd worn every Sunday since she first walked through those very doors. Alfonso knew he could never be like the Daddy Too Muches of this world—he'd never been the kind of man who could go to America and pluck a wife like she had been cultivated just for him, and he would never be the kind of preacher who would amass the power to bulldoze longstanding structures so he could have a place. He had to tell Inimfon this, tell her something. But they had a service to prepare for. He found a second rag and proceeded to wipe benches.

———

When it was 8 A.M., Alfonso positioned himself behind the lectern and waited for the door to swing open. After a few minutes, tired of standing still, Alfonso began pacing the length of the hall, and did so for the entire thirty minutes of

Sunday school while Inimfon sat quietly. Ncobody showed up. Alfonso reminded himself that it was not uncommon for members to skip Sunday school and turn up only for the main service. But by 9:20 it was still just him and Inimfon in the room.

The silence stretched on for so long, Alfonso thought it would snap. "We should start the service," he said finally. "The Bible says that where two or three are gathered in His name…"

Inimfon shook her head. "Alfonso, there's nobody here."

Alfonso stepped away from the lectern and joined Inimfon on the bench where she sat. It creaked under their combined weight.

"I went to see that new church," Alfonso said, without looking at Inimfon. "Sister Boma was there… Brother Ifeanyi."

"I've been trying to tell you."

This was the time to acknowledge all the things she'd been trying to tell him, and to tell her the things he needed to say, things he needed to repent from—his silences and resentments, the shadow that his pride and ego had cast over their lives.

When he finally opened his mouth, it was to make a flaccid joke, one rendered sour by its proximity to truth. "Maybe I should come and be a serving boy at your restaurant"—he gave a weak laugh—"since I don't have members anymore." He expected Inimfon to smile, respond with a counter-joke, and then some reassurance, something blandly benign, like "It is well," or "God is in control." Her answer was a noncommittal "Hmm."

Alfonso wondered why it was so much easier to talk to an unseen God than to the person beside him, made of flesh and blood, like him. But people were capricious, and prayer was a shield. He would ask God to soften Inimfon, make her recognize his essential goodness and the repentance in his heart, without him having to grovel or debase himself before her. Alfonso bowed his head and closed his eyes. He didn't move when he felt the air shift beside him, but his heart sang with gratitude; Inimfon was getting on her knees to join him in prayer.

Alfonso heard the door creak, and when he opened his eyes he was alone. He found Inimfon minutes later, seated in the car, her hat tossed to the floor of the back seat. He got in beside her and turned the key in the ignition, filling the space between them with shaking.

THE SECULAR AND THE SACRED

Frances Elizabeth Kent was born in Iowa, in 1918, one of six children in an Irish Catholic family that moved to Hollywood when she was a child. At eighteen, she took the name Sister Mary Corita, entering Immaculate Heart of Mary, a Catholic religious order known at the time for its progressivism. She studied art at Otis Art Institute (now Otis College of Art) and the University of Southern California and learned serigraphy from Mariá Sodi de Ramos Martínez, the Oaxaca-born screen printer. As head of the art department at Immaculate Heart College in Los Angeles, she stressed collaboration and emphasized the art-making process over the result. "You have no distinction," she told students, "between what is art and what is not art. You do everything as well as you can."

Her work was widely popular—she was on the cover of *Time* and *Newsweek*, and those she influenced range from John Cage to LA's Self Help Graphics & Art, founded in 1973 by one of her students, Karen Boccalero. But her teaching career coincided, controversially, with the Second Ecumenical Council of the Vatican, or Vatican II, reforms intended to modernize the church. Embracing the

call, her students radically blurred the line between the secular and the sacred. When the art department took over a Mary's Day celebration at Immaculate Heart, they used the bright, graphic language of advertising to conflate the exuberance of the marketplace with rebirth and joy: their snapshots served as

inspiration for a Fluxus-like happening. The local bishop reprimanded Corita Kent, deeming the work as frivolous, to which Daniel Berrigan, the activist poet and priest, responded: "She is not frivolous, except to those who see life as a problem. She introduces the intuitive, the unpredictable into religion, and thereby threatens the essentially masculine, terribly efficient, chancery-ridden, law-abiding, file-cabinet church."

By 1968, Corita Kent left her order,

A Mary's Day banner: "Nothing is real to us but hunger"; pictures made in grocery stores, for graphical inspiration; art from advertisements.

concerned, in part, that her celebrity inhibited her collaborations. She moved to Boston, where she was offered a position at Harvard but instead became one of several teachers at a community art center in Cambridge called Project, Inc.
—Robert Sullivan

—

Tim Devin, a Boston artist and archivist, has mapped 1970s countercultural organizations in the Boston area in his pamphlet series Mapping Out Utopia, *excerpted here, beginning with Project, Inc., where Corita Kent practiced after leaving Los Angeles.*

1. 141 Huron Avenue, Cambridge
Project, Inc. / Project Arts Center
This was the second location of Project, Inc., an art school founded by artists Celia T. Hubbard and Rita DeLisi in 1962 and offering classes to children and adults. Its teachers, all practicing artists, included Corita Kent, whose work Hubbard exhibited at the Botolph Group, a Boston gallery that showcased contemporary religious art. In the early seventies, Paul McMahon presented conceptual art shows at the site, during the school's off hours, featuring artists ranging from Laurie Anderson to David Salle to Dan Graham. By the midseventies, Project's classes had expanded to include ceramics

and photography, its name changed to Project Arts Center.
Years at this location: 1963–1984 (or 1987, depending on who you ask)
Current use of building: commercial (high-end clothing boutique)
Current value of building: $2,245,500

2. 188 Prospect Street, Cambridge
Boston Area Ecology Action / Greater Boston Ecology Action Center / The Store
This was the second location of Boston Area Ecology Action, after it moved from 925 Massachusetts Avenue. Originating in Berkeley, California, Ecology Action was a nationwide network of environmentalists, where members practiced what would now be called creative activism, holding mock award ceremonies, for instance, to get media attention for ecological issues. The group opened an organic food store known simply as The Store at this site. It sold food in bulk, with minimal packaging, which could be returned to the store for reuse. The Store also formed a partnership with a 150-acre organic farm in New Hampshire, making it a precursor to many localist food ventures in the area.
Years at this location: mid- to late 70s
Current use: no longer standing (now a 7-unit condominium)
Current value: $5,094,000

Above: Los Angeles, a Mary's Day celebration. Below: Boston, Corita Kent's kitchen.

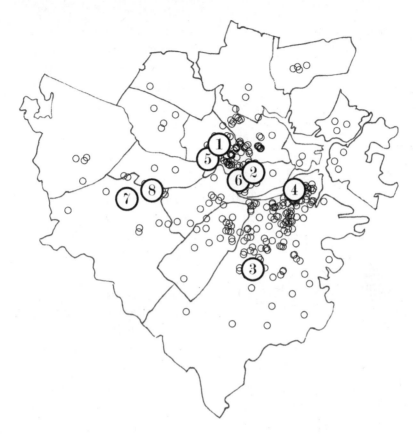

3. 6 Marmion Street, Jamaica Plain

Cooperative Artists Institute

CAI was founded in 1970 by African-American artists and musicians who saw the arts as a way to build community. It operated as a co-op, members sharing administrative and creative duties, each member receiving the same living wage. The organization produced art events around Boston and published *Artists in Residence Journal*, which, according to *Communities* magazine, was "a resource sheet to stimulate exchanges of ideas within the arts community." This was CAI's first headquarters and the collective household for four of the thirty-five members. CAI reorganized as a multicultural organization, aiming to "empower people to solve their individual and collective problems by applying the arts as a catalyst for personal and institutional change."

Years at this location: 1970–?
Current use: residential (3-family house)
Current value: $575,300

4. 70 Charles Street, Boston

Beacon Hill Free School
In the early 1970s, during an alternative education movement in Boston, small "free schools" sprung up across town, offering free classes taught by anyone who could come up with an idea that would draw a crowd. At the center of the movement was the Beacon Hill Free School, based out of the Charles Street Meeting House at 70 Charles Street.

Years at this location: late 60s–70s
Current use: commercial (offices, stores)
Current value: (not in assessors' online database).

5. 16 Lexington Avenue, Cambridge

Cell 16 / No More Fun and Games
Cell 16 was a radical feminist group that was "committed to confronting issues, such as self-defense for women, equal distribution of housework, consumerism, birth control, abortion, childcare, the media's portrayal of women, and guaranteed minimum pay," according to Northeastern University's archives. They produced a journal called *No More Fun and Games* and ran their own martial arts school, the Cell 16 Tae Kwan Do School of Karate. This was Cell 16's first location, before they moved to 2 Brewer Street and then onto 14a Eliot Street.

Years at this location: late 60s–early 70s
Current use: residential (2-unit house)
Current value: $2,780,000

6. 46 Pleasant Street

Women's Center / Women's School
In 1971, on International Women's Day, Bread and Roses—"an organization of socialist women," according to their founding documents—occupied an abandoned Harvard University building for ten days, declaring it "The Women's Center" and demanding equal opportunity for women in America.

With a $5,000 donation, the group bought the house at 46 Pleasant Street, creating a permanent women's center, to address "a pressing need for information, resources, and support to fight the discrimination women experienced," as their website puts it. Still in operation today, it offers free classes, therapy, job coaching, and housing assistance, and continues to publish a newsletter begun in 1971.

The center was also the home of the Woman's School, offering classes on "anti-racism, auto mechanics, growing up female, international women's struggles, lesbianism, Marxism, older women, and many other topics," says the center's website. The longest-running feminist school in the country when it closed in 1992, the Woman's School was all volunteer run.

Years at this location: 1971–present
Current use: Cambridge Women's Center
Current value: $721,800

7. 811 Washington Street, Newton

Voice of Women / The Peace Boutique
At Voice of Women, a peace organization
that protested nuclear weapons and the
Vietnam War, members led teach-ins,
sit-ins, and street demonstrations, and
canvassed for antiwar candidates. They
also ran the Peace Boutique, which sold
antiwar crafts and materials; all proceeds
went to "promote peace and combat
repression," according to the 1971 edition
of *People's Yellow Pages*. During their
height, VOW had about three thousand
volunteers working on various campaigns
and programs.

Years at this location: 1960–1973
Current value: $6,150,000

8. 474 Centre Street, Newton

Interfaith Community Peace Center
The Eliot Church founded this center
in 1963 to provide office and meeting
space for antiwar organizations, including:
Non-Violent Direct Action Group, which
supported draft resisters, at one occasion
blocking buses bringing draftees to their
physical exams (1963–?); Clergy and
Laity Concerned about Vietnam, which
lobbied the Catholic church to take a
stance against the war; the Honeywell
Campaign, a national campaign to hold
the Honeywell Corporation accountable
for the cluster bombs and anti-personnel
weapons they supplied to the US Army
during the Vietnam War (midseventies);
and the *Newton Times,* a women-run,
alternative weekly newspaper focusing on
the peace movement (midseventies)

Current use: a preschool
Current value: $4,723,000

COLUMBO AND SUGAR OKAWA

Around 8:30 every night, it was dinner. From the recollections of their three daughters, dinner was the grandest, most pleasurable thing Columbo and Sugar Okawa ever experienced. Dinner was like watching actors perform a scene. A scene in which a family had been starving for six hundred years. Salt, sugar, and animal fat had been utterly unprocurable in their land.

And then it was like one of the Okawa children, probably Yuki because she was always wandering about with her crummy eyesight, stumbled upon a forgotten door in the family's apartment.

And when the Okawas opened the forgotten door, there was a table laid with a meal so succulent and juicy that Columbo and Sugar began to rock and tremble and sob and even pee-pee in their pants a little bit.

"O zowie! O wee wee! This is magnificent stuff!" Columbo would roar, in a voice deep and incredulous, holding up his dish of noodles and hominy casserole and examining it from every angle. "What do chefs in France call this? In Lyon? In Marseille? I would like this on my next birthday. If the ingredients are not too rare, I would like this as my Christmas dinner!"

"O golly gosh! O giddyup!" Sugar would cry, stabbing her fork into a brothy plate of Spam, stewed tomatoes, and scrambled eggs. "I once ate this same food in a dream! In a childhood dream! How did you do this, Daddy? A great husband and cook? How did I get so lucky?"

"My loves, my loves, my loves, my loves, can you believe we get to eat such a delicious bowl of food?" Columbo would ask his children, digging into a potato and pea chowder, making a show of dabbing a thin paper napkin at the corners of his mouth. "I'll bet Napoleon never tasted anything this good. Not even on his wedding day. Your mother is somewhat of a pioneer, isn't she?"

One cooked, the other hyped the children. Columbo and Sugar were equals in their cooking abilities, and they were not what anybody could call good at cooking. But they knew how to produce a meal at a sprint. They could cook one-handed with a small child perched upon their hip. They could somehow chop, flip, mash, and serve all with the same long metal serving spoon. From a mostly empty refrigerator emerged full family meals the week before payday. Sauces were mayonnaise and one other thing whipped together, usually shoyu or ketchup. They cooked from canned and bagged and boxed foods. If one of them boiled fresh ears of corn or steamed some green beans, it was an occasion for much wailing and clapping of hands and prostrating across the dinner table.

"It's absolutely yummy, Daddy. The cuts must've been pricey! How do we afford such incredible flank and shank?"

"I told the butcher I was making Sugar Okawa's birthday dinner, and he threw the shank in for free! Apparently, you are something of a celebrity in this city!"

The more gruesome their days at the Strawberry Mountain Jam Company or the Sweet Star Prunes dehydration plant or the Momotaro Frozen Peaches factory, the louder and more insistent their enjoyment of the meal. If they kissed their daughters' heads as they entered the room, if they kept inventing reasons to get up, return, and kiss their daughters' heads again, it meant they had been yelled at repeatedly by a supervisor. Days they praised the honesty and good standing of their daughters, days they dreamily speculated on their daughters' future successes, were days their hands were covered in bandages. If their meal had been divined through a hodgepodge of double coupons, if the protein was scant or mushy, if the broth was more salt than bone, if the forgotten bake was disastrous, the grander their proclamations became.

"Merlin's silver chin puff! Who did this banana bread with the rice cereal and Keebler Fudge cookies baked into it? What a stroke of wizardry! A mortal man made this? Daddy, tell him I must marry him at once! Tell him I say!"

"O but you shall be disappointed! I am afraid this man is blissfully married already to a remarkable woman. And with three marvelous children!"

"But I must have him! Tell him I shall murder this wife and these children of his! And then he will be mine!"

Some nights the Okawas chomped loudly, moaning, with their eyes closed. Sugar said with food this good she lost all control of her eyelids. Sometimes Columbo fell asleep at the table, and his children would lay their napkins across his back like little blankets.

Nothing bad or annoying could happen at the Okawa dinner table. If one of the children knocked over a glass, and it shattered, well, that glass had always been bad luck, had always made the lemonade reek like sulfur. Now they were freed from its curse! Freed! Retrieve the pith helmet and excavate the freezer, Daddy! A coffee mug of the finest black cherry ice cream to the girl who vanquished the glass!

"O my goodness, the baby's head seems to be bleeding, Daddy!" Sugar once exclaimed at dinner.

"Of course it is, my love, my love!" Columbo said. "I trimmed her nails this morning, and now she seems to have the razor paws of a badger."

"Trim her nails, the more deadly she becomes!" Sugar bellowed. "We truly are a family of warriors!"

Outside the boundaries of dinner, the Okawas were a pretty regular couple. They undercut and bickered and cold-shouldered. A handful of times, the Okawa children witnessed Sugar slap Columbo's face. On one particularly strange Thanksgiving, the girls watched Columbo drag a wooden dresser of Sugar's clothes into an alleyway and obliterate it with an ax. But then, outside dinner, it was rare to see both of them in the same room at the same time. Columbo worked two jobs, Sugar worked three. And if they weren't working or eating dinner, they were drying dishes, inspecting groceries for mold, or driving to the laundromat.

The Okawa family did not eat at restaurants. Why eat at a restaurant? They were overrun with mice and insects on this side of Oyster Ridge. The hosts always seated the Okawas along a dim back wall near the restrooms. The waiters always got their orders a bit wrong, subbing in a scant or more expensive plate. And wasn't Sugar's cabbage and peanut soup the finest in the city if not the world? Wasn't Columbo's saltines-in-place-of-bread pudding incomparable to any desserts of their land? Some nights the Okawas did spread a pink-and-white fringed tablecloth in place of the teal PVC-like covering that was usual. The pink-and-white tablecloth had to be hand washed, whereas the teal covering was like a raincoat that only got a wipe down from time to time.

The Okawa dinner routine lasted years. The enthusiasm and optimism sustained until the end. The end was after fifteen years of dinners, at which point Sugar and Columbo separated. The separation was well timed. By then the Okawa children spent almost all of their free time with their friends. They often skipped dinner to do homework or watch television or fool around on the computer.

The separation happened in spring. The weather was glorious. The streets were covered in dewy blossoms. Tomiye was nearly in community college since she had skipped two grades. Yuki was starting high school. Kaji was starting junior high. Even the children themselves agreed the separation was well timed.

The Okawa children grew older and got married and had their own children. They were close, but not too close. They called each other about once a month. They called one parent or the other about every week. Either it was a call or it was a voice message. Or it was an envelope stuffed with useful coupons leaned against the door.

When the Okawa children each arrived and departed from their forty-second year, they were individually struck by how peculiar the age felt. Forty-two. Forty-two was how old Columbo and Sugar were when they divorced. When the children spent time together—a major holiday, a funeral—they often found themselves saying things like, Jesus, they were so freaking young at the time. No wonder Mom and Dad were so clueless. They were just freaking kids that whole time.

After Columbo Okawa died, the newspaper printed his obituary using his legal name of Kimi Okawa. The mortuary's online announcement misprinted his name as "Kimi Okinawa." Few people had ever heard Columbo's legal first name, and almost all of his acquaintances missed the funeral in the confusion.

After Columbo died, Sugar dropped her nickname and even went back to using her maiden name. For five years she tried pretty hard to make a go of her life as Shizue Sugai. But if she was being introduced by a friend to somebody new, she was usually introduced as Sugar Okawa. She settled on the name Sugar Sugai for her headstone. This felt like a good compromise. It wasn't right next to Columbo's headstone, but it was pretty close by.

When the girls came to the cemetery on the same day, they could kind of spread themselves out four or five feet apart and pretend the plots were united. Kaji would be looking down at their father's headstone and Tomiye would be looking down at their mother's and Yuki would be sort of squinting back and forth at her siblings. The Okawa children would stand that way for a while, trying to reenergize their tenuous connection. They would stand without saying a thing. They were so still and so quiet the Brewer's blackbirds and the cliff swallows and the rust-colored towhees perched nearby to observe. And the house crickets lowered their thorny limbs. And the orb weaver stopped devouring its meaty wasp atop the stabilimentum. And all the mourning cloaks rested, and all the moths awoke early.

And then one day Tomiye died. And then Yuki died. The Okawa grandchildren lost jobs, some divorced spouses, some remarried, some grew fortunes, some gathered dogs, some lived lonely miserable lives.

Until she died, Kaji's children visited her in a place called the Oyster Ridge Nursing Home. Kaji's children arrived at 11:15 A.M. and stayed until Kaji's lunch was delivered. And then they excused themselves, saying, "Have a nice lunch. We'll see you tomorrow, Mom."

Though Kaji's children lived in the same city as the nursing home, they typically only visited their mother once in a month. Always arriving at 11:15 A.M. Always excusing themselves when lunch was delivered.

One spring day when Kaji's lunch arrived, she reached out and grasped the hand of the young man who delivered it.

"O wowza! O golly gosh! What is all this fancy stuff? Is this recipe from the Amalfi Coast? You must've trained as a chef in San Gimignano!" Kaji exclaimed. Kaji pumped the young man's hand in a couple of victory squeezes.

"O god!" the young man said, taken a bit by surprise. "I will tell the kitchen you dig it. I'm just a volunteer."

Watching him go, Kaji said quietly, "Yes, please, my love, my love. Tell the fine man who made this meal that I must marry him. I must. I must. I must. I must."

And that was the last thing Kaji's children remember her saying.

THE METAPHOR GAME

Everyone in class is scribbling furiously. The topic on the board: "Love versus Hate." We're about to begin *Romeo and Juliet* and the timer is ticking down toward the last two minutes. Now something's wrong with Rafael.

"My head hurts," he mumbles.

I squat down next to the mass of black wavy hair and whisper, "Maybe you're dehydrated. How about a trip to the water fountain?" Rafael suddenly sits up and arches back until his black tee reveals a band of pale skin, just above his black jeans. He shakes the hair off his cheeks. His mascara has smudged over his right eye.

"Go on. Grab a drink of water."

Rafael swivels out of his seat. "What's with the *agua* imagery?" He waggles his lip ring with a finger. "What am I to you, Joseph in some parched desert in Canaan?" I know Rafael's head aches partly because it's literally painful for him to read and write. He's dyslexic but also the most intellectually curious in the class; thanks to the glut of graphic novel versions of the classics, he's the most literate. Plus, he's great at The Metaphor Game.

"You're a beached Greek boat," I suggest, "waiting for wind."

"You're the Grim Reaper, penciling kids their fates." He winks and snaps off a shot with his index finger, peering into my eyes with a weird pity. It's the same look Crispus gave me just before I drowned him in the bathtub.

I euthanized Crispus, my two-year-old Rottie, about a month after he jumped out of an Uber on the Major Deegan. We'd been sitting in the stifling car for about thirty minutes in traffic around Yankee Stadium. Two cars hit him before I dragged him to the shoulder. The vet said he'd need expensive reconstructive surgery. For weeks, I carried him down four flights twice a day so he could hobble around the newly planted gingko saplings on the Grand Concourse and do his business.

Rafael's headaches arise from various sources: from his Dominican grandparents, with whom he's in constant battle; a school system that makes a sixteen-year-old dyslexic freshman, starting his third high school, sit at a desk six hours a day; the two cute K-pop fangirls who visibly flinch when his bulky shadow skulks by them out of the room.

For our creative writing project, Rafael's working on a manga version of Odysseus's encounter with Circe. In his retelling, his dad, currently serving time in Dannemora, struggles to get home to Mott Haven but gets waylaid by a sexy drug dealer outside of Troy, where Rafael's mother is now in rehab.

I had never killed an animal before. So, like when my fridge broke or I needed to know how to broil salmon, I found online videos describing how to euthanize a pet. Rafael was the only person I told. In retrospect, that was a mistake, but I felt he would understand the immensity of the dilemma. He confessed he had once watched a kosher butcher's video demonstrating how to slit a cow's throat so it didn't feel any pain. He offered to share the URL.

After our last class before Christmas, Rafael stopped in and slipped me a couple pieces of folded loose leaf. He looked me in the eyes until he was sure I was listening. "It's my final masterpiece."

While our teacher-student choir caroled "Dona nobis pacem" in the hall, I read Rafael's story. It described the narrator, who always wore black, glorying in a revenge slaughter with a machete and bottle of hydrochloric acid of a class of ninth graders, complete with exploding eyeballs, sheared ponytails, severed tongues.

I knew Rafael would never hurt a living creature. I also knew he'd just read the manga version of Sophocles' *Ajax*. I recognized a metaphor when I read one. But these are the end days of literature. Literalism rules.

I shared Rafael's story with the principal, copied his guidance counselor and the social worker. Two weeks into January, I was told Rafael had been officially transitioned from our school roster.

There are several DIY ways to put down a pet. Apparently using a gun is most common, like Candy's dog in *Of Mice and Men*. But I don't live on a farm so I chose drowning. Why not have my vet euthanize him? I guess I felt obligated to use my own hands, and I wanted him to know how much I loved him.

MAPPING WHY WE WRITE

There are poems that allow us to be what we are, or what we want to be, without shame. Poems that harness and manifest dignity within us. This is what I've always taken it to mean when someone points to a "permission-giving" work of writing: seeing someone else like you, writing with grace about the same things that consume you. These five poets—Angela María Spring, Huan He, Yasmine Ameli, Ann-Marie Blanchard, and Maja Lukic—each of them immigrants—extract dignity from the processes of upheaval and change that necessitated their or their families' movements. *Permission*, in this sense, feels closer to its etymological origins; *mission*, to send, as in entrusting a task to an ambassador. We can see a distance form within the word *permission* itself, an ocean or a sky; and to what end does the poet serve as an ambassador, crossing this space?

A map delimits space and may even depict the shape of a poet's territory; a map can also take us through history and the evolution of language, as we see in the etymological explorations of "The Language Map": "words eke out a scrap of my ancestral map / all Latinates con tinny church bell / peal of sameness of any conqueror's language."

Does the poet here serve as an ambassador to a place that now only exists in ancestral maps? The poet's work becomes a slow piecing together of Latinates and "Indigenous teeth." A mapping of languages lost, forgotten, or otherwise subjugated under the hegemony of the "conqueror's language." The poet, now more akin to an emissary for spirits long past, sounds their church bell until finally a poem is achieved that will remind us now and forever of our histories.

And if not in the past, where can we continue our search for dignity? In "Bury My Tongue," the map's landscape creases with grief, and in the wrinkled folds, we find ourselves "broken by distance." "They will bury the babies and my goddaughter will stand at their baby-size grave. / Tomorrow, my tongue will run aground."

Often I have thought of myself, and the immigrant experience as a whole, in terms of shipwrecks. Whatever was lost in the map's crease, our language, self-esteem, culture, the dead babies whose faces we won't see in person—now wrecks drifting to the bottom of the sea—the poet-ambassador has made it their mission to retrieve those losses through this poetic act. The tongue running "aground" like a beached ship. A tomorrow met with grace.

THE LANGUAGE MAP

ANGELA MARÍA SPRING

What is a *country*

Origin

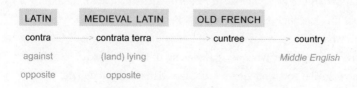

LATIN	MEDIEVAL LATIN	OLD FRENCH
contra ——→	contrata terra ——→	cuntree ——→ country
against	(land) lying	Middle English
opposite	opposite	

lying opposite
passive voice against
a territory

LATIN	LATIN	
terra ——→	territorium ——→	territory
land		late Middle English

terra sounds like *terror*
or la terreur *en Français*

so what is a treaty
a sweet *treat* to shove
between Indigenous teeth
whiskey and high-fructose
dreams draw down pull the guns

LATIN	LATIN	OLD FRENCH	
trahere ——→	tractare ——→	traitier ——→	treat
draw,	handle		negotiate
pull			Middle English

out to negotiate what is a nation
born from a culture qué es una cultura
English /   Spanish /   French
words eke out a scrap of my ancestral map
all Latinates con tinny church bell
peal of sameness of any conqueror's language

On one side
Caesar cuts a swath
through Gaul to return with echoes
of their gods   glistening new
Roman faces and one deity   identity
lost to time and mistranslation and unwon

wars becomes "the Celtic Mercury"
so scholars argue among themselves
in unread papers whether France
harbors a cult of Lugh
                    shining light
like a refugee in his own home   land

On the other side four thousand years
before one doomed man crossed la Rubicón ridículo
the Lokono pushed sturdy canoes off the shores
into a new beginning   sin

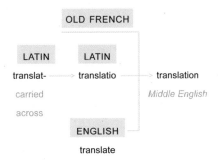

THE YELLOW IRIS

HUAN HE

I.   Flood the riverbed on the curse of a
cattail, jealous that a boy in rain boots
scooped up his lover, the yellow iris,
who stopped his prairie watch only to
help a limping grasshopper. Storm clouds
gossip about this tall tale of yearning, their
gray hairs pinched modestly, unheard by the father
lost in a fly-fisher's spell.
A spotted toad skips between the boy's legs,
darting through green-yellow weeds
into the mouth of a splash. The boy, Ming, strokes the
tip of each cattail with two palms, a rickety plane desperate
to take flight. The yellow iris, behind his ear
in companionship, surveys the wide bend
of the Platte River. Wounded skies make room,
a gesture of welcome despite
the dead buried in the Sand Hills.
He remembers the lightning, the thunder,
reaching down to see if the earth remembered too,
this time, or the next. Flooded, wet, soak up
the new rain that painted his eyes in only gray,
no color could escape. Running, the yellow iris kisses
the sunburned mark behind his ear
before becoming the wind.

II.   The rice fields shine like rows of tinsel,
       the sun a neighborhood beggar in a lazy nap.
       A boy, who will become the father,
       drops a candy wrapper. The villagers from Shaoshan
       stomp its pink out, rushing to see the sky swallow the
       flight of cranes. Over the low rolling river, the birds slip
       in between the folds of summer heat. An old stick balances
       on the neck of a sunken man, his walk that of mud,
       passing the boy, running on the earth-skinned road toward
       the white cuts of lightning. He lifts his head skyward,
       and rain takes the shape of a boy.

MERCY

HUAN HE

A tribute is

a wish made public, and I salute you,

O you soldier;

stationed in

mouth, I hold still like field mice, huddled

in a red barn

raised to be

a church. Is heaven what you swallow,

or is it the opposite

of mercy? A

boy had to learn to fish by becoming an

iridescent bobber

at once a

pearl and a poison, wearing the averaged

face of a Walmart

sticker. In

the pulse of you, I see the night drinking

the fire. A prairie

is a holding

ground for sinners on their way to the forum;

the tunnels lead

not to

respite but to each other, shapes out of air.

CHILDHOOD BIRACIAL

YASMINE AMELI

At the liquor store, I trace the *S* on a bottle of *Shiraz* while my father chooses a wine to bring to dinner. I am more than a decade too young to drink, but I ask for the bottle *because Shiraz is in Iran and I am Iranian* until he says *No* and studies my face, my error so obvious to him. *You were born on American dirt.*

My father repeats *You are not Iranian. You are American* until I consider that my mother might not be my mother. I study my complexion in the car's side mirror. *You think that you are Iranian?* he asks. For the first time, I see that I am in my father's likeness: the sun-streaked hair, thin lips, unhooked nose.

My mother might not be my mother.

When we return home with the white wine, she irons the bust of my Norooz dress stiff for Easter dinner. She complains that her sister-in-law *pretends Easter matters more* while I scratch at the tulle and the tights.

I memorize her face for our resemblance: an arched brow, a dark ring around the pupil.

My father dabs on cologne, calls my favorite uncle *lazy*, Iranians *lazy*. I narrow my scope to the television and flip through the channels in search of a Charlie Brown Norooz special that will never materialize. My toes rub against the tights' seams until the itch makes me clench my muscles.

When Ramine steals the remote, I scratch his skin red until our father blocks the television and Ramine returns into my palm the remote control, useless to us both.

We will say anything to discard our father from the scene: *I started the fight. These welts are my own doing.*

BURY MY TONGUE

ANN-MARIE BLANCHARD

You don't know what it's like to have twin deaths in the family, to sob from your bedsit in London, where the sky is so gray it births grief like ailing pigeons. Don't you know I'm broken by distance? My friend, Aussie, postfeminist, ran from her family. Why, she says, didn't you run at birth? She lost her accent only to regain it from exhaustion. I'm losing my family. Baby deaths. Baby burials. I'm remnants. Remains of a teen, troubled, remains of a child, sling necked but alive. Tomorrow, they will bury the babies and I won't be there. They will bury the babies and my goddaughter will stand at their baby-size grave. Tomorrow, my tongue will run aground.

YUGOSLAVIA: *THE ENCYCLOPEDIA OF THE DEAD*

MAJA LUKIC

New quinces line old streets
in an old place I know as new.
When I write this, I'm in Belgrade.
September apples spoil in the grass
and no one collects them.
I've been pressing old currency
between the pages of recipe books.
The bills lie there like strange
flat flowers attending paper
funerals, blue-and-purple
mold spreading over caskets.
I'm not hungry, only tired,
and it's too late to find my city
or my street in it. "The place I'm from
is no longer on any map."
Once I stopped being a Yugoslav,
I was ruined from being anything else.
I keep aging but Yugoslavia never does.
Our monuments fall into disrepair,
decay grows on us, becomes our skin,
the ideologically disoriented lot of us.
And now memories are so slip.
The Internet overlays my slim archive
with a random YouTube repository
of videos and grainy voices,
radio static and state TV,
old concerts my parents attended.
Everything is out of order
or in its own particular order—
my mother is a teenager,
she reads President Tito's
birthday greeting at

a Youth Day celebration,
thousands listen to her;
Lee Oswald shoots JFK
and my grandfather in Croatia
turns off Voice of America radio
and never listens again;
umbrellas spin in the rain
at a train station while waiting
for the Blue Train carrying
Tito's coffin; little children set
flowers on the tracks, then
dart back to their parents' hands;
Jimmy Carter's mother steps off
a plane in Belgrade;
masses of dignitaries swarm
Tito's funeral, and a young
Saddam Hussein pauses at his coffin
longer than anyone else;
in the factories, the workers
have stopped at their stations because
they know the country is over then—
not before and not after.
But these are not my memories—
I was not alive for the first
Non-Aligned Conference in 1961,
though I would have liked to be.
I did not watch those Winter
Olympics in Sarajevo's snow,
though I was once afraid of snow,
the first time I saw it on
a mountaintop in Bosnia. I was little,
raised on the Dalmatian Coast,
and never having seen snow
before, terrified of so much
whiteness obscuring the landscape.

I understood it to be a kind
of sea, not solid, and believed
there must be snakes beneath.
I learned later that, of course, there were.
Particulars are crucial in
The Encyclopedia of the Dead.
As Danilo Kiš taught us, every life
is sacred, and to that I would add,
even the brief life of a nation,
even when one is born late
into its gruesome, dying years.
Someday, the last Yugoslav will die,
and I would like it to be me.
I realize this is a morbid wish.
Not long ago, I met a man
from ex-Yugoslavia but I knew
I didn't love him. I was only
homesick. These days,
I confuse love with nostalgia.
I sit at a museum and watch
a slideshow of my vanished state.
A friend tells me South Slavs are
not usually melancholic like me.
So what is wrong with me?
I click through videos of student
protests; worker protests;
Milošević, deathly nationalist,
with his massive head;
and there, too, is Tuđman,
with his tiny fascist eyes, re-creating
a Croatia I never wanted;
old promotional tourism videos; police
beating protesters; and old flags
shimmering in Partisan-era
domestic films. I watch *Walter*

Defends Sarajevo over and over,
tanks moving left and right,
someone else giving a speech.
In the later videos, the war years,
there are crowds but no collective,
there are masses everywhere
but stripped of brotherhood and unity.
It never ends differently;
it never ends at all, in fact.
Both over and not,
both dead and infinite,
our old country continues,
spills into media and air.
It's as real as poverty and
the ruined faces of new refugees
(now from Syria, now
the war is elsewhere)
at the bus station in
downtown Belgrade.
Yugoslavia is as real as
Death to Fascism,
Freedom to the People—
the only slogan worth knowing.
For as long as I can write it,
Yugoslavia exists, but I could
never write it back into being.
Linden leaves fall on my hair
on some warm night and
everything scrambles again.
Fruit dissolves into brandy,
graffitied swastikas cartwheel
along bridges in my birth town
in Croatia, and I stand in the square
of an old city—call it Belgrade—
where a little girl plays a violin.

Its coiled sound loops into
a sky of rain and military planes.
It sounds like I'll never rest again.
Or I go to sleep in the House of Flowers,
thinking of my mother, while
someone strokes my hair,
and I remember that Miljković wrote
"And even if they were to kill me, I love you."
The truth is, the years reflect back on us
badly. The future came to us first, and
everyone said we were barbaric.
Now the whole world is barbaric.
And I—I come to systems at their twilight,
just before they fall apart.
Lately, I suspect I'm the cause.

NINA AND THE LIME

Nina has just gotten off shift and onto the ʀ, still wearing her issued T-shirt with the slogan "Workers of the World, Unite!" emblazoned on the back. Once she would have changed before leaving the shop, but lately her boss had been questioning why she'd been staying later and later, even after all the closing tasks were complete and she'd clocked out. ("I get a notification when the café doors actually lock," he'd told her, gesturing to his phone, "for security purposes." He was wearing a face of concern. "Are you okay?") The stench of day-old coffee grounds lingers in her wake. Her fingers tap-tapping away at her phone are dried out but she really doesn't feel like stopping at Rite Aid and grabbing a small bottle of moisturizer. Dim lights, long commute. Service flickers in and out for the umpteenth time and she drops her phone in her lap, annoyed.

The subway doors gape and close with a lurch, moving her and her fellow commuters farther, deeper into Queens. Nina picks her phone up again and opens Gmail. *I want full custody of the lime*, she writes. *Happy to talk over the phone about this. But I want full legal custody.* She gives the email a once-over and presses Send.

It doesn't take him long to respond. *What do you mean*, he writes back. *Are you okay Nina?*

She mulls over the repeated question as she makes her way back to the apartment she shares with two other girls, both also service workers, though one is a bartender and the other sells phone plans. Are you okay, Nina. It seems to her the least pertinent thing to ask, out of all possible questions. The phrase wriggles into her bones, into whatever is left of the lime's being, the placenta and the rot.

The lime was named thus for its size when Nina and her ex realized its existence. Nina thinks it's an it; her ex disagreed and pointedly refused to use pronouns whenever the lime was brought up in conversation, *not like we could know their gender anyway*. They had been dating for *three years* (four and a half, Nina had quietly corrected him after dinner with her parents. *What?* Four and a half, Max, not three. We have lived together for three years, but we started dating while still in college. Max had stared at her. *What's the difference.* There are miles between three and four and a half, she thinks now, like the difference between a lime and an orange, the difference between a paid-for degree and a diploma bought with student loans, or the difference between what the lime would be now and what the lime actually is). "Your little one is now the size of a lime, weighing about half an ounce," she'd read from her then-unbroken phone, as Max lay next to her in the bed they had once shared, wrangled from the Ikea in Red Hook. "She has reflexes now, and soon will curl her fingers and toes, clench her eye muscles. Her—stop poking me, Max, it's not funny—her intestines will move back into her stomach area? This is insane."

He had stopped poking her abdomen and instead rolled dramatically over the side of the bed, colliding with the nightstand, his glasses clattering onto the floor. Down on one knee he had gone, arms flung toward her. "I guess this means I must marry you, you who are bearing my fruit," he had warbled. Even now when she thinks about this scene, the inauguration of the lime, she can't help but let out a smile.

"I suppose," she had sung back. "Did my parents put you up to this? Marriage by dint of child born out of wedlock?"

Max grimaced. "Sure. I'm sure your dad would love to know that a white ghost knocked up his only kid and therefore ensured said white ghost's surname would get passed on instead."

"Come back," she had patted the cooling dip in the mattress, and he had slipped back into her arms, just like so.

"Well, what are we going to do with the lime?"

She doesn't remember his expression or even his tone; she had turned her face to the scarred ceiling. "What do you mean, what we're going to do. We can't have it."

He stayed silent, head resting on her chest, their breathing going out of sync. She had read some post as a half-baked teenager that said *bringing their respiratory systems in alignment* would *deepen the connection* between her and her dearest, another way to *ensure that their souls were in communion.* The post got upwards of thirty thousand likes. She still notices whenever a boy falls deeper asleep, breathing growing slow and steady.

"We don't have money for a kid yet, Max." She spoke into his hair, a shock of chestnut. "And I haven't made anything I'm proud of yet. I don't even have a show," she had started up in a growing panic.

Once upon a time he had known her from the inside, could feel the twist in her stomach whenever she got anxious; once upon a time she could sense the hitch in his throat across the room. But that was a literal lifetime away. "You could film the lime being ripped out of your uterus," he suggested, pulling her closer. "I think that'd be a win with the *Artforum* crowd."

Nina rolled her eyes but couldn't help laughing. "Yeah, sure, I bet they would love a critique of bloody, compulsory motherhood."

He slipped out of bed again, this time for his nightly ritual: heating up the bowl with a small blowtorch, scraping a bit of murky green wax with a sculpting tool she once used for her clay figurines, and inhaling the sweet smoke of *flower* (it was always *flower*, neither bud nor weed but sometimes *marijuana*). Of course he came back into the bedroom after a long while. They fucked but Nina no longer remembers exactly how, and she doesn't want to feed any false memories. The one thing she does remember is how she had let herself touch her stomach, a ginger, careful touch, while Max was dabbing. A lime nestled within her flesh, she was enveloping her lime, she had been all along for months before she had even known.

I just want full control over—she stops and deletes the sentence. *I want to take full responsibility for the lime. It was mine before it was yours.* She deletes the latter part, then decides to reinstate it. *The lime is not your redemption arc. You don't get to have*—

That's not what she means to say at all. The bartender is out and her Sprint roommate is blasting Khalid, a sure indicator that she has brought home a boy and is having *the best sex of her entire life*, earrings jingling for emphasis. She is nineteen. Nina closes the door to her sparsely furnished room, deletes the whole thing, and rereads Max's terse email. *Are you okay Nina?*

She starts there. *I am completely fine, thank you for asking. I just want to start my life again, this time with a new vantage point. It will just be the lime and me.* She hesitates, but decides to add a couple more lines before hitting Send. *The café is hosting some of my new paintings. Let your friends know.*

Max, to his credit, responds right away. *Whatever you want. Whatever makes you happy. I have no interest in advertising your fruit canvases. Let me know if you need help with money.*

Always the one with the last word in any argument they had. Nina impulsively presses Reply. *I don't need your money to buy the lime joss paper.* She mutes the thread.

The first clinic that had an opening was on Staten Island, nestled in a two-story building on a slope curving into faux colonial buildings and a brand-new shopping complex. The consultation was uneventful. They had gone on the ferry together first thing on a Saturday. Nina had wanted to pretend that they were on a date, as if they had just met in college at a mutual friend's "experimental" film screening and had decided to go to Governors Island together. He had been quiet the entire trip, even moody, repeating that he respected her decision, that she, after all, was the one incubating the lime.

Seated in the sea-green room, the kindly gynecologist explained the procedure. Terms like *dilation* and *curettage* and *local anesthetic* were deployed for a while until it was clear neither understood what she was talking about. "The procedure involves opening up your cervix and scraping some of the tissue out of your uterus." The gynecologist opened her clasped palms. "It may cause some cramping, but you'll be back to normal in no time."

It was enough to convince Max to not take the day off. She took the 8:30 A.M. ferry for a 9:00 A.M. appointment, sending him cheerful texts about her upcoming performance piece.

They settled her in a chair, with a glowing screen pinned to the ceiling depicting sakura flowers. She really isn't sure if she was placed in that room because they clocked her as an Asian girl in need of consolation. But she immediately appreciated the flowers, the delicate folds, as they forced the nub inside her to open, sucked at her insides with what looked like a vacuum cleaner in miniature. Every sound reverberated in her ears, almost muffling the shriek of her uterus, all its cramps magnified. There are five petals to a cherry blossom, Nina chanted to herself. There is a kindness to cerulean. Even from her reclining position it wasn't as if she couldn't see the lime inching up from her vagina to an opaque tube to a cylinder. A clatter on the floor indicated that she had dropped her phone from the chair. Her hands, she realized, had been gripping the chair's sides.

She thought of fruit, of a grapefruit split open with a cleaver, pulp, the thirst of a man hungry for water, for the juice of a lime. Sourness filled her mouth.

The wound inside of her pulsated whenever she moved; the over-the-counter painkillers they had given her waned every several hours. From the couch she saw Max taking a hit from a bong. He offered her a hit. She passed.

For a while it was just the three of them, the lime only coming up unbidden, otherwise a benign presence in the apartment. Max took more of an interest in scrolling through LinkedIn late at night, easy-applying to jobs she had no idea he took an interest in, until one day he finally landed a copywriter gig for a generic erectile dysfunction medication subscription start-up. Less avant-garde art, more tastefully arranged bananas and oblique references to not being able to get one's penis erect. Nina had no idea what to make of it. Max would come home after office drinks chattering about VC money, MTA campaigns. She puttered on with her shifts and empty canvases, often too tired to draw or paint when she got home. "Maybe you should think about getting some other job," Max commented near the end, stepping over several scattered tubes of gouache. "One that won't ask you to carry things in excess of fifty pounds."

Nina pretended to not have heard. She focused on the little ridges of the sheet of weighted paper in front of her, pale as eggshell. There was nothing she wanted to paint or make, save for the occasional fruit-themed illustrations popping up in her head fully formed. Her nails making little indents in a citrus rind—she found herself oh so resistant to the idea, but found herself painting the scene anyway.

After a small lunch on Mott, she walks past a small store selling craft sets of paper cigarettes, Maseratis in miniature, papier-mâché houses with servants looking down from balconies. She impulsively walks into the store, catches a glimpse of all the different sets of joss paper, bright-gold squares surrounded by cream. Folding ingots is a material way of demonstrating how much you honor your ancestors, she thinks. Can you ask your ancestors to protect someone not even recognized as part of the family's lineage? Was the lime, a descendant nullified, now an ancestor? She finds herself imagining a sculpture of a lime made from joss paper. She walks out.

———

"I'm doing this for you, you know," he had said in one of their last fights. "For us. No one likes having a nine-to-five. You're the one who said that we didn't have enough money."

"Enough money for what?" she screamed back.

Max paused and looked at her. "Who do you think?"

"If you bring the lime into this, I swear to God—"

"I think"—the cud of his words spilled onto the rug as he picked up the half-finished hand-in-fruit sketch—"you're too selfish to be a mom."

Ma, she starts a new text, deciding to bypass the family WeChat. *Do you know if people burned joss paper for dead kids? Like, actual babies. Babies who don't make it past the first hundred days. Babies who haven't been named yet.*

Nina would have googled it but she's rusty at Pinyin. Not like she would know what to put in anyway. "Dead child paper money"? She doesn't remember the words for *practice, custom. Chinese for folkloric practice*, she types; the iMessage notification pops off. Her mother is up, it seems, probably playing mah-jongg. *I'm not sure, peapod*, Ma writes. *I think we burned some ingots for Auntie Huang's ancestors, asking them to protect the little one. Why?*

It's for an art project, she writes back. It is the default answer to most of her mother's questions.

The bubble floats above her keyboard. *It's disrespectful to use the dead as a hobby, Ling-ya. I hope we've taught you better than that.*

She stares at the phone for a little. She wonders if the lime would have had a Chinese name. Googles *lime in Chinese. Sour-orange* and *green-lemon* stare back at her. Will there ever be a lime without a modifier in front of it? She switches back to the text chain with her mother. *Don't worry, I won't.*

In this life Nina now picks a small can of baby formula from the supermarket, pouring half into a jar, which she will use as an incense holder for the rest of the year. The 7 rumbles past her apartment's rooftop, tiny emptied bottles of Fireball and New Amsterdam littered all over. Into the can goes a tiny sweater she had knitted around a lime, with sleeves that hung awkwardly from the sides. Into the can goes a note that says *Your incubator loves you* in her neat handwriting.

Several origami cranes made of gold-flecked crepe paper in next, an emptied box of animal crackers. With a lighter she had stolen from Max, she sets an origami heart alight, dipping the flame to the rest of the lime's belongings. There go the crackers, now the sweater too. Once the fire reaches the citrus peel, it sizzles, flares up, the oils fuel the starburst of color. She hopes it means the lime got its stuff, wherever it is. Eventually the evaporated milk powder puts out the flames, and with that, Nina begins to cry.

DREAMWEAVER

I. Rodger doesn't offer to take me to the train station and I don't ask. I call for a car. The driver speeds relentlessly on the highway but I'm too nervous to say anything. I'm not going to tell this guy how to do his job, even if not doing so gets me killed. Instead, I tense up in the back seat and worry about the day of travel ahead, if I make it that far.

It's an hour by car to the station, a short train ride to the border, a few hours to get through customs, and then a five-hour train ride west, followed by another hour's drive to the house. I loved the trip when I was younger, watching the landscape change the farther west I went past the border, land churning up little waves of hills that dissipate into still, inland flatness. Now I am full of dread.

I recognize the woman across from me on the train almost instantly, though she hasn't looked up from her lap long enough to really see me, too absorbed in shrinking into herself. Most Othersiders are, on this side, and I know her eyes slide right over me precisely because I'm not actively trying to disappear. For a moment I debate saying anything to her, a silent, uneventful ride to the border appealing to my anxiety. But I can't say nothing to her. We were friends for a long time.

"Tabitha?" I ask, leaning across the aisle to get a good look at her.

"Matilda?" she whispers, looking confused.

"What are you doing here?" I ask, cheerfully, before registering the blinking bracelet on her arm. A company tracker.

"Going home," she says, glancing. "You?" she asks without looking up at me.

"Me too. Going home."

I become aware of the oppressive quiet in the train car. I lean back into my seat. We do not speak for the rest of the ride.

When the train pulls into the station, everyone stands to retrieve their bags from the bins overhead. In the moment of commotion, I lean back over to Tabitha.

"What happened?" I ask.

"Got caught working," she says quietly. "They dragged me out of the house and said I was saved from being trafficked."

She's radiating anger. People ahead of us are beginning to file out of the train car, our moment to talk evaporating before I can gather my thoughts. Without thinking, then, I grab her hand and squeeze. She squeezes back.

Agents are waiting for her on the platform.

Customs is even more of a nightmare because now they recognize me from my dreams. A man in a shiny red-and-white uniform looks at my passport, looks at me, looks at my passport again, and calls over a coworker.

"Look at this," he says. "Matilda Rove."

The other man looks me over, appraising me, doing his job. "Come with me," he says. "You've been flagged for a screening."

I set my jaw. He takes my bag and leads me through a steel door to a long hallway, more doors lining the walls as far down as I can see. I'm ushered into a room and when the door closes, sound from the outside world seals off. The thunk of him chucking my bag onto the table between us makes me wince.

"Please, sit," he says.

I sit.

"For an Othersider," he says, "you seem to have done remarkably well for yourself."

I shift in my seat, say nothing.

"Did you bring the machine with you?" he asks.

I play dumb, though of course I knew better than to bring the Dreamweaver. "What machine?" I ask.

"The one that lets you see your dreams," he says sharply, annoyed.

"No, sir," I say.

"Do I have consent to search your bag?" he asks.

I know if I say no he will search anyway. "Yes," I say. "Go ahead."

He unzips my bag so slowly that I hear each tooth unclench. He takes his time looking through my things. Thankfully the bag is small. Some shirts, an extra pair of pants, my underwear. I do not react when he shuffles through my underwear. I have nothing to hide. When that becomes apparent, he zips my bag back up.

"Well," he says, sounding a bit disappointed. "You are cleared to proceed."

He leads me back the way we came and just before he closes the steel door, he encourages me to break up with Rodger.

II. "Can I get a *whoop whoop* for active shooter training?"

Daniel paced the wall of the staff room with an unnecessary microphone, fluorescent lights shining on his shiny spots: his forehead, his cheeks, his slippery thin lips, and, when he turned to make another lap, the gap in the hair on the back of his head.

I let out a meek *whoop whoop*. I was too new at the company to be outwardly disaffected, but there long enough to know I wouldn't be making any friends by coming off as overly enthusiastic. I held a Styrofoam cup of lukewarm hot chocolate close to my chest. Undissolved granules of cocoa floated on top with the marshmallows. I was staring into my drink, eyes fuzzing out, boring into it, *boring, ha ha*, I was thinking, when I heard my name called over the speakers propped up at either end of the room.

"Matilda! Matilda Rove! Tilly—get up here!"

Hands nudged me to the front as Daniel made a loud sound into the mic that fractured into shards of feedback, celebratory, somewhere between a *yeehaw* and a *yaas*, both of which I'm sure he knew he couldn't pull off.

I stood sheepishly, the hand that wasn't holding my drink in my pocket, out of my pocket, flattening the front of my shirt. My coworkers looked at me. I didn't look at them. I looked at Daniel, who was maneuvering a large, long box covered in a cheap plastic tablecloth to the center of the prize table with a bit of flair. Daniel and I made eye contact, a look in his eyes that I couldn't quite read. I shifted my weight back and forth from foot to foot, fighting an urge to run.

"Well," Daniel said, savoring a delicious moment of anticipation, the attention in the room that had been wavering all afternoon finally and fully back on him. "We almost didn't do this today. But, you know, I thought, what the heck. Some excitement never hurts, and we've all been working so hard. Matilda. Tilly. Congratulations—best prize of the day!"

He whipped the tablecloth off the box with all the flourish of a magician. Beneath the tablecloth, a Dreamweaver.

A Dreamweaver.

I felt the bottom of my gut go out and I said, "Whoa." *Whoa*. Not what I was expecting. A new device, maybe. Or a Keurig. I don't know. Not a Dreamweaver.

Daniel handed me the long box and I held it awkwardly beneath my arm, not thinking to set my cocoa down, trying hard not to spill and growing increasingly pink in the face. I became aware of a sort of surprised applause from my coworkers; they were clapping hesitantly and with reverence.

The end of the meeting slipped me by. I was too shocked to pay attention, feeling the box snug beneath my damp armpit. When I made it back to my desk, Dodie cornered me before I got a chance to sit down.

"Oh my God, Tilly," she said, eyes tracking the length of the box. "If you sold, you could, I mean, you could walk right out of here and not come back for—I don't know!"

I knew. The thing was worth just short of my yearly salary. It wouldn't be worth that much in six months, after it had been on the market for a season, and I knew already a 2.0 was in the works, but still—

"Yeah, I know," I said to Dodie, "I know. It's crazy."

"Are you gonna use it?" Dodie asked, eyes swinging up from the box to my face.

"I don't know. Probably. I mean, I don't even usually remember—"

"All the more reason!" Dodie said, clapping her hands together like a child, a gesture I'd never seen her make before, glee emanating off her in waves. "Oh, you've got to. You've got to! Use it tonight! I want to hear all about it," she said as she stepped out of my cube, her gaze lingering on the box until she finally turned to leave, the shape of her wiggling and undulating away past the pixelated glass.

Many days passed before I opened the box. Inside were two compartments, one holding the long, slender processing unit, the other holding the cap. It occurred to me then that the branding for the Dreamweaver was so sleek because the machine itself wasn't, exactly—there was something medical about it. I had read that the technology was originally developed for therapeutic uses, but so far design had failed to erase this clinical, utilitarian origin. At least they had gotten rid of all the wires and plugs for the commercial release.

I placed the processor on our bedside table. Encased in a hard, white material I couldn't readily identify, too sleek to be plastic, too warm to the touch to be metal, it had a small glass screen at one end, with the iconic power button below the screen. I reached for the cap. It was slippery and fleshy, opaque, cum colored, with little sensor nodes dotted evenly around. The cap had an uncanny feel to it, as if made of something animal, flayed skin. It was moist to the touch but left no residue on my hands. It made me shiver. I slipped it over my head, as instructed by the little pamphlet at the bottom of the box.

I pushed the power button, which lit up in a gentle periwinkle color. I stood to look at myself in the mirror mounted above the dresser. I waited for the cap to sync with the processor—when this happened, the sensor nodes on the cap lit up in the same perfect pale purple, light undulating softly. I felt deeply apprehensive.

Rodger came in at that moment and laughed at me.

"What?" I asked, defensive, annoyed.

"Nothing, but it's a funny color, don't you think?"

I didn't answer, shrugging instead and turning to crawl into bed.

"So that's that?" he asked.

"What's what?" I asked, still defensive.

"You just go to bed? With that on your head? That's it?"

"Yes, Rodger," I said emphatically, annoyed because that was obviously the way it worked. You put the thing on, you hit the button, and it records your dreams all night.

"Well," he asked, squinting at my head. "Does the light fade eventually?"

"Yes. As I fall asleep. It says somewhere, hand me that," I said, pointing to the pamphlet in the box. "Yes. Says here. 'Color scientifically calibrated to provide optimum sleep conditions. This color has been proven in our laboratories to induce vivid dreams.' So there you go, yeah? The color turns off when I do."

"Optimum sleep conditions?" he asked, eyeing the twinkling periwinkle coming from my head. "It's a bit bright, is all."

"Yeah, well, I'm not really tired," I said, tossing the manual off to the side of the bed, moving to make room for him. It took both of us a long time to fall asleep, but I know Rodger fell asleep first, because I watched as the pale light reflected on his face slowly faded.

III.   "Now what?" Rodger asked.

"I get ready to go to work?" I said, slipping the cap off my head, trying to find somewhere to put it down. I wished I had a wig mannequin. I hung it off our bedpost. Rodger looked grossed out.

"Aren't you dying to watch?" he asked, nodding to it, dangling there.

"I'm really not, Rodger," I said. He looked offended. "I'm sorry, I don't mean to be rude. I just—I bet it's all just long stretches of black, anyway. And I have to get going. And I think there's like, a three-hour render time, and I'll be at work and you'll be on campus, so," I said, trailing off. Rodger didn't believe me about the last part, that the processor had to render. I showed him the manual and his shoulders slumped.

"Okay, fine," he said, and I had to laugh at his boyish excitement.

"It'll have to wait until dinnertime, okay? We can have a viewing party," I said. He looked cheered up by this. "I'll even get the good popcorn," I added.

Work was maddeningly slow. I hunkered down into the corner of my cube where I was least visible to passersby. I found myself checking the time on my device every few minutes, aching to get home to watch the footage, dreading it, too. It was difficult to stay present, fidgeting, paranoid and alert to every footstep, afraid to be caught doing nothing. I resented myself for this depravity and lack of productivity.

I had sent my proofs to Daniel the week before, knowing full well I wouldn't get comments back from him for another few days. In these situations, Daniel told me to read industry news, to stay current on what was happening, and to keep a close eye on the language used in the press, to focus on the writing in particular. I never considered myself much of a gamer and I never had a firm grasp on what the thing I was working on meant, exactly. But Daniel believed I possessed the capacity to fake it.

"As long as you sound like you know what you're doing, you know what you're doing," he told me shortly after I was hired, a friendly bit of advice that revealed more about him to me than I think he'd meant to admit.

Purely out of fear, I eventually got around to trolling for things to parrot. I hated it but, I have to admit, Daniel was right—and I was good at it.

I ran into Dodie in the staff room at lunch. She was wearing these amazing red boots, sleek and soft and shiny and leather, with a perfectly substantial heel, no unnecessary hardware—it drives me insane when boots have useless embellishments, like a buckle on a boot with a zip up the side. I admired them openly as she stood at the sink, washing out a mug, my takeout leftovers buzzing around in the microwave.

"So, how's it going?" she asked, breaking the silence of the room, drawing out the vowels in her sentence to hedge around the awkward atmosphere.

"Oh, pretty good, I guess. You?" I asked. My voice sounded too loud.

"Good. Good. You been using it?" she asked. I could feel myself flush. I hated that this was what she always wanted to talk to me about. Her first question was always to get my attention, the next question about the fucking Dreamweaver.

"Yeah, actually," I said, trying to modulate my voice to disguise any annoyance, "used it last night."

Her eyes zoomed in on me, hungry for any details. "Oh yeah?" she asked. "Anything crazy happen?"

"Haven't watched it yet," I said, being completely honest with her for once.

"Oh," she said, shoulders slumping, and she continued rinsing out her mug. I could see I disappointed her. I wanted to talk about something else.

"I like your boots," I said, sincerely.

She looked down at them, turned them in the light.

I man a paddleboat in from the ocean. The dock ahead, at the foot of a tall city, is a massive spiral. I steer my craft in tighter circles until I reach the center, where I disembark. Then I walk the dock, undoing the spiral on foot until I am at the outer edge. I dive into the water and swim to shore. Dodie's boots sit seaside, like she's kicked them off to go for a dip herself. I scan the beach for her, then the waves—no sign of her except the shoes.

I wear Dodie's boots into the woods. The ground is wet and squelching. Everything is wet and in flower. I regret wearing her boots because they aren't functional, I keep slipping, and I'm getting them all muddy, ruining the beautiful red leather. I try to step gingerly and fail. The woods grow thick. I push brambles and branches out of my face, breathing desperate.

I part the overgrowth and before me is a stream. Above, the canopy of trees is thick but light trickles in, shafts pointing to the water. I approach. The water is clean and clear, flowing gently, shallow. I scoop some to my lips to drink. I follow the stream. In places, the water branches in two, making way for little islands of sand. I walk along the sandbars in the middle of the stream. I stub my toe on something hard. I bend, looking, and clear away the sand beneath where I stand. A mask, half-buried, made of mother-of-pearl—I pull it up and out, turning it in the beams of light from above. It could be my face.

IV.   I sleep for most of the train ride to Grenada, the town where I get off and meet Mother and Valentine for the last leg of the journey. It feels strange to sleep without the Dreamweaver. I can feel where the cap should be, holding my head. I miss the smell of it, slightly rubbery, and I can't get comfortable, wadding up my coat into a lump to use as a pillow against the window. I drift across the landscape in an in-between kind of haze, neither here nor there, thoughts drifting like they're dreams but always a little too closely tethered to reality to truly stretch into images. To stretch into sleep.

Mother is weepy at the train station. Valentine claps me on the back. I feel dehydrated, like I need to take a shit. We pull out of the station in Dad's old green truck. As we drive, I find the change in the landscape totally jarring, how flat everything is, how low the buildings are, everything in sight colored tan like the dust in the road and the fields and the buildings and the sky. Between Grenada and Lamer is a shallow valley, so that when you leave one town to head toward the other the road dips in a long straight line from the nose of the truck. Lamer is visible from a long ways away, the grain silos looming like castles. Smoke, too.

A tall plume of smoke, rising in the distance. Valentine, driving, growls under his breath and shakes his head. My mother tightens her grip on the armrest but keeps up conversation like nothing's happening, asking me about Rodger and work and what is this thing with the dreams. Valentine is driving fast, we approach the fire that seemed far ahead faster than I expected. Fire on the side of the road, licks of flame eating through a field of tall, dead grass, black smoke churning into gray as it rises. We can feel the heat in the car.

"Someone must've flicked a butt," Val mutters. In his voice, jealousy. Cigarettes are hard to come by.

There are fish in the pond.

"Let me introduce you," Mother says, pointing eagerly at the water. "We've got Daffodil, Lazy Hazel, Sunshine, Helen, and Spots," she says.

"Spots is still alive?" I ask.

"Oh, no," she says, patting my arm, "this one is just also named Spots."

Entering the house is strange. It's not the house where I grew up. Mother moved when I was in college, into this house, a smaller house with a bigger yard on the edge of town. But everything from the old house is there, all the furniture, the smells, the kitchen knives. Of course it's all there, I know that's how moving works, you take your possessions from one place to another. But I find it unsettling in this house, all these childhood associations cropping up in the wrong place.

We eat, we drink, and I sleep a deep dark sleep.

I wake to the sound of a peacock screeching in the yard, the sun barely up.

The peacocks are feral, descendants of pets let loose generations gone. They tend to stick to the fields and the yards of the houses that border the fields just outside of town. The birds know which backyards have dogs, which have gardens. Most of the yards are empty and dry. The peacocks hop fences by feebly flapping their enormous wings.

The long tail of a male disappearing behind a building, a flash of blue where none is expected.

v.   "You don't talk about it much," Dodie will say one day, touching my hair.

"It's hard to talk about," I'll reply.

All around is softness and warmth, the smell of Dodie fresh from the shower, her skin tacky against mine as we lie in her bed.

"My dad died during the war," I will admit. I'll stick my chin out. There, I said it.

"What happened?" she will ask, her voice small and sad and warm and supportive all at once. I will feel an intimacy with her I've never felt with anyone, like I could tell her everything and at the end of it we'd still be there together, safe.

"He was too old for combat but he worked in a field office. Supply chain management or whatever, making sure food was going where it needed to be. And," I will say, feeling depths of feeling I haven't allowed myself to experience since it happened, a sensation like the terrain beneath the bed is shifting, swirling, gaping open, "the company bombed the office. Or tried to bomb the office. It landed next door in a field. Dad had a heart attack."

Dodie will squeeze me with her entire body, pressing her face and legs into me. For a moment, we will be still. The gaping maw beneath the bed shudders shut.

"Isn't that a crime?" she asks.

I shrug. "Well, they didn't do it, did they? The company is very good at what the company does," I say. "It would be a crime if a person did it. And if they hit their target. If the directive came from a single source, you know. But it didn't. You know how the company is. It's diffuse. It's everyone."

Dodie will nod against my chest. For a moment longer we are still.

"What about you?" I'll ask. "You never talk about it either."

She will squirm, roll onto her back, stare at the ceiling. "I had just finished school. I didn't want to fight, but because I was in the optimum physical wellness age bracket, and because I knew I had to work at the company after, I had to do something. So I was a nurse."

I turn to look at her, trying to imagine her in a nurse's uniform.

"I was terrible at it," she'll say. "I was fainting like, every day. Toward the end I was mostly emptying bedpans. That's how I met Daniel, actually."

I look at her incredulously. "Daniel fought?" I ask.

"Oh, yeah," she says, her eyes going wide. "You didn't know? He volunteered for the front. He was a real sick fuck about it, from what I hear."

VI. *I am unsteady as my father and I climb to the lip of what he calls the Black Hole, a quarry turned swimming hole. The water is deep and still in winter, not frozen but giving the impression of a gelatinous black mass. I don't know why we hiked up here. Nothing else to do and the day is clear. But my knees feel weak, each step laborious to set down. I tell my father I feel like I am going to faint and then I feel as though I am waking from sleep, strangely comfortable, splayed on the rock with my father bent over me.*

"Is this a dream?" I ask my father.

My head hurts when I wake, dehydrated, it's so dry here, but I think there's something else going on. My head—more like my skin, really—aches where the cap goes at night, I can even feel the shape of the nodes in flashes of pain. My mother gives me a hot compress, a cold compress, a back rub, a worried look.

In town, there's nothing to do. Most of the shops on Main Street are closed and the ones that aren't are sparse. There's the movie theater, but it only has two screens and both are playing movies that came out two years ago on the Flipside. There are people here I know from childhood, high school, but I am so alien to them it's impossible to keep up a conversation. I end up spending a lot of time in my parents' house, and when I'm not doing that I'm walking the edges of their property, out to the trail that runs a circle around town. Yesterday, I found a horny toad. It blinked at me and flicked its tongue before darting into taller grass. Today, I found a nest of peacock eggs in the seat of an ancient, rotting truck. It's not the season for laying eggs but I don't blame the birds for thinking so. I touch one, cold as a brick. The fragile shell breaks from the slight pressure of my hand. Black yolk runs over my fingers. I hold my hand up to the light to inspect the slime. Satisfied by what I see, I wipe my hands off on the seat of my pants and turn to walk home.

VII.   My mother and I disagree.

"You can't show my dreams to anyone here," I tell her, vehemently.

"But you're so talented! You've been so successful on the Flipside. Wouldn't it be nice to be successful at home, too?"

"It would be dangerous," I manage, weakly.

I suddenly know. A dream. My mother's face comes into sharp relief. She's been speaking and I cut her off. "That's all well and good, Mom, but it doesn't matter. I'm asleep."

Her face falls slack, the version of her I'm seeing my mind make.

"What do you mean?" she asks.

It's hard to look at her face because I remember how angry I was in the dream. She senses something is off and tries to smooth things over by giving me small tasks to do, this being the big day, the holiday. I get out her dry ingredients from the pantry in the basement. I run a rag over all the flat surfaces in the house. I feed the fish. I chop the apples. My mother intuitively knows what I have not yet figured out for myself: doing something makes everything better. By the afternoon, I've relaxed. I'm halfway looking forward to the parade.

———

Wind whips around the corner of Main Street where we stand, taking my hair with it in wild directions. I'm so distracted by trying to get my hair back in order that I don't see the start of the parade coming down the street until it is nearly on top of me: rows and rows of tanks, soldiers in red and white with guns at their sides, marching in time. The crowd is silent, faces watching.. These tanks fought in the war. These soldiers fought in the war. They stream along for what feels like forever, a testament to what little damage was done to our side, all these tanks made it, all these men lived! I find the whole thing disorienting and dull, one uniform blending into the next, one horrific machine after another.

When the veterans have passed, the party begins. Trailing the tanks and soldiers, clowns at the ready with streamers and confetti, candy and horns. The crowd cheers, children push to the front to grab at the beads and balls thrown into the crowd. I take a chocolate from a man wearing a blue wig. There's even a horse.

My father's truck drives by, hauling a float of flowers in the shape of a house on fire, a symbol for the start of the war.

On the way home, my mother walks slowly. I see her so clearly. The wind has died down and the sun strikes her face, shimmering and golden. Looking at her is almost too much to bear.

"I think I have to go back to the Otherside early," I say.

"Whatever for?" she asks.

"Work," I lie.

My mother is my mirror. When we stand this close, infinity explodes between us.

SMOKING CIGARETTES
IN WEST TEXAS

Arnold spoke with a thick tongue, in a drawl that's dead now. He meandered around words and then sometimes stopped—midsentence—to make sure you had both eyes on him. I didn't like what he had to say, but I loved to hear him speak. I wanted a voice like his and all the confidence that came with it. Waitresses often mistook him for an actor or a country singer they couldn't place.

Arnold didn't like bad manners or stained teeth or lazy opinions. He didn't curse, and he didn't like people who did. He said "good night" instead of "goddamn" and "so help me Hannah." He rinsed his gray hair brown with a solution that smelled of bitter almonds. The scent clung to his hair, his skin, his clothes, his car, and eventually our house, our clothes, our hair.

My mother met him the same way she met all the men she dated—at a bar off I-10 with my aunt Cass and Cass's then husband, James. Arnold cut in when she was dancing with another man, and his confidence impressed her. Unlike the other men my mother danced with that night, Arnold never fumbled the turns, or lost the beat, or crushed her toes. He slipped one arm around her waist and led her across the floor with a firm grip. Then he led her out to the parking lot. Dancing with Arnold reminded my mother that some men still knew how.

When my mother came home late that night, she tore around the house and turned on every single light. From the dark of my bedroom, I heard her shuffling around the kitchen, laughing to herself, bumping into things. I heard cabinets flung open and the clink of glass hitting the counter as she poured herself one last drink. Light from the hallway crept into my room and then swung into my eyes as she knocked open my door and tiptoed in, drink in hand. She crouched by the bed. "Scoot!" she whispered.

Her breath stank of cigarettes, but I liked these conspiratorial moments. I could imagine my mother the same at fourteen, crawling into bed with Cass in my grandmother's house to whisper secrets across pillows.

"Roe," she said as she lay her head on the pillow facing mine, "I met a man tonight."

Before she passed out on the stash of mystery novels in the bed with me, she told me all about him; she described his broad shoulders and thick brows and how delicate he made her feel when they danced. As she spoke, she ran her hand through my hair. "He didn't like that crack in the windshield," she murmured. "But he says he's going to fix it—he says he's going to fix everything."

"What do you mean?" I asked, but her eyes were closed. She had fallen asleep, her fingers still in my hair.

As it turned out, Arnold intended to fix everything by breaking my mother of her bad habits. Like skimping on car repairs and smoking cigarettes and letting me run around town with a bowl cut and a lazy eye.

He didn't care that smoking killed you—no one in west Texas in the late eighties really believed that anyway—but he thought that smoking made women look witchy. He'd roll up in his red truck to where my mother and the other nurses had gathered around a tall plastic ashtray outside the hospital and shout "What's brewing, ladies?" I don't think anyone but my mother ever got the joke.

I didn't expect my mother to give in. She wore other people's impressions lightly. She held up long lines at the supermarket, fishing wads of coupons out of her purse, to purchase forty jars of shrimp cocktail or a year's supply of powdered lemonade. She washed her panties in the sink and hung them out back to dry, even though our yard wasn't fenced in and the neighbors could see. If she was hungry during Mass, we stood in the back of the chapel passing back and forth a noisy sleeve of plastic-wrapped doughnuts. Only certain things shot through the cracks—like when my aunt Marie, my mother's religious sister, would say something snotty about me never growing out of my tomboy phase. My mother said Marie's comments didn't bother her—Texas women didn't all have to parade around like pageant girls. But on Sunday, I'd find my mother on all fours digging through my closet, her head eclipsed by a pile of loose clothes, searching for something feminine to shove me into for church.

Maybe she wanted Arnold to stick around because she'd grown tired of dating younger guys who listened to bands she hated, who spoke like they were from somewhere else, who weren't Catholic anyway. Or maybe it was because Arnold had this effect on women. They acted dead drunk around him, giggling and slurring their speech, leaning in toward him like they wanted to tell him a secret. It might have been his unnerving scent or the way he carried himself like an echo of John Wayne. Even I felt it, and I never sought the praise of men unless they were the gatekeepers of high marks or essay contests with cash prizes.

I knew Arnold wouldn't disappear as quickly as the rest when jade-colored bottles of Dr. Wendell's Dark Hair Tonic materialized around the rim of our tub. He started joining us for dinner.

"Hey Rosie," he'd say over dinner, "try to keep your lame eye on my fork."

"It's not lame. It's lazy."

"Eye over here," he'd say.

No one ever called me Rosie. I went by Roe. Rosie sounded too velveteen, whereas I was made of elbows and angles. Soon after Arnold came into our lives, I'd started overhearing my mother dropping Rosie into conversations with her sisters on the phone. Even though she's the one who started Roe, who never called me anything else. When Arnold complained about my eye, she'd say, "We're getting it fixed when she turns sixteen," but it always sounded more in her defense than in mine.

Arnold stopped making a show of getting in his car and driving around the block as if he were headed home after dinner. He started picking me up at school whenever my mother or Aunt Cass couldn't. By the spring, he was snatching cigarettes out of my mother's hand every time she tried to light up.

"I want to quit," she said, "but what the what am I supposed to do with my hands?"

That's when Arnold came up with a so-called genius plan to have his sister Janine teach my mother every hairdo known to womankind, from tightly coiled curls to a french crown. That's how Janine quit smoking, or so Arnold said, as Janine hovered nervously on our carpet, clutching a tiny pink suitcase stuffed with hot rollers and bobby pins and fat cans of AquaNet. She was as slight as Arnold was imposing, a bony thing with wispy hair and pursed lips, nodding her head as Arnold spoke, not so much agreeing with him as bobbing in his wake. I studied her porcelain skin, stretched tight across her face. She didn't look like an ex-smoker to me.

Many Sundays in a row, Janine came over and my mother and I sat on the yellowing carpet with her, the room smelling of burnt hair and chemicals, as she showed us how to do an updo in the time it takes for the stoplight to turn from red back to green. I wore my hair too short to do anything but comb it, so I held a hand mirror for my mother and Janine to see the backs of their heads. Arnold supervised from the corner and said, "If she looked like a lady, it might distract from that lame eye."

By the summer, my mother rarely smelled of smoke, and with all this new blood in her brain, she started taking on extra shifts at the hospital. One afternoon, a few hours after we'd dropped her off with two french braids running down her back, she called to say she'd be home late and could Arnold fix something for dinner? Well, Arnold didn't cook, and I couldn't cook meat—which was just about the only thing Arnold ate—so we got into my mother's car and drove to Dairy Queen.

On that long stretch of paved road between our house and a chocolate milkshake, Arnold slammed on the brakes in front of the Salvation Army. I thought we had stopped short to avoid hitting a stray dog or cat, but as I spun around in the passenger seat, looking for an animal running off the road, I saw what he saw—a crushed velvet dress with a deep-purple bodice and tulle skirt slung over the mannequin in the window.

"Whooeee!" Arnold shouted, jerking the car into the parking lot.

Arnold headed into the stucco building and I followed him. Opening the doors to the showroom, I noticed the teased blond wig flopped over the mannequin's head. Arnold spotted it too. It wasn't for sale, but Arnold walked over to the register and smiled at the salesgirl.

"Kelly," he said with barely a glance at her name tag, "could I trouble you over that wig in the window—that beautiful blond one." He pointed behind him without turning around. "I know it isn't for sale, but I'd love to buy it for my daughter."

That wig reeked of church upholstery and the dress came wrinkled, but as soon as the salesgirl handed him a receipt, Arnold told me to go into the changing room and put both on. I didn't want to, but I didn't protest—at fourteen, I didn't know how. "Don't you look darling," the girl said without taking her eyes off Arnold when I finally came out. I held my T-shirt and jeans in a heap under my left arm, and with my right hand, I tugged at the puffy sleeves, trying to smooth out the shoulder pads. I looked up at Arnold, careful not to move my head too quickly. For the first time since I'd known him, he smiled with all of his big white teeth. "Let's go surprise your mother," he said.

Arnold threw my real clothes in the trunk, and we drove off to kill some time before heading to the hospital parking lot. Hours passed. With the car radio on and the windows open to the cool evening, Arnold began to sing. His deep voice lulled me into a kind of hushed state. I almost forgot where I was until I felt his fingers poking into my ribs, prodding me to get out of the car and wait where my mother could see me.

I looked like a ruined prom queen standing there beneath the streetlamp in an otherwise dark lot where doctors and nurses slept in their cars between shifts. When my mother finally came out of the hospital, I wasn't sure she had seen me until I felt her hand reach around my wrist and drag me from the spotlight to our parked car where Arnold stood, a satisfied grin on his face.

I think he thought she'd praise him. I don't remember much about what was said. She yelled and maybe Arnold yelled back or maybe he just stood there, mouth open and dumb, as she swiped the keys from his hand.

"You better get a ride home tonight," she called out the window, plunging the car into reverse.

We drove in silence, slipping through the night, until we rolled up the gravel drive in front of Cass's house. I stayed in the car while my mother slapped the door with flat palms and twisted the knob until her sister appeared behind the screen in a long ratty nightgown. My mother pointed, and I watched Cass lean out to get an eye on me. From her squint, I couldn't tell if she was disgusted or just couldn't see me clearly. My mother waved me over while Cass ducked back inside and flipped on the kitchen lights, flooding the yard with shadows. "Now I think this is just as ridiculous as you," my mother said on the front steps before we walked in, "but Arnold's got my camera, and I think you're going to want to remember this."

"You look like goddamn Miss Texas!" Cass shouted.

The next couple hours smudge in my mind in a happy, hazy way—like when something gets you just right, and you laugh so hard and for so long that you forget what made you start. In all the places I've ever lived, I keep the photographs we took that night in a shoebox under my bed. A shot of me in that creepy wig and itchy dress pulling a half-eaten roast from the fridge. A shot of me tangled in all of the telephone cords Cass owned, holding two receivers, one to each ear. A shot of me holding a carton of milk like a trophy, pretending to cry. Aunt Cass snapped the photos, and by the time we fell asleep on the living room floor, all three of us were stomach sick from laughing.

My mother nudged me awake around 6:00 A.M. She needed to get back to the house to change before her next shift. On our drive home, a pale pink cut through the sky. It spilled into the car and cast a warm glow on my mother's faded uniform. She reached under her seat, fumbling for something, finally unearthing a crushed carton of cigarettes. She slipped two into her mouth and with one hand lit both as the other hand eased our car to the side of the road. She exhaled loudly. Without moving her head or shifting her gaze, she passed one to me, and I took it with both hands. Time stretched and split in those few minutes of silence as we blew smoke out the window. I'd never felt so old or so young.

CONTRIBUTORS

Yasmine Ameli's work has appeared in *Poetry*, *Ploughshares*, *AGNI*, and elsewhere. Based outside Boston, she holds an MFA in creative writing from Virginia Tech.

Kiik Araki-Kawaguchi is the author of *Disintegration Made Plain and Easy* (1913 Press) and *The Book of Kane and Margaret* (FC2/UAP). His story in this issue was edited by Megan Cummins.

Ann-Marie Blanchard's work has appeared in *Meanjin Quarterly*, *Salt Hill Journal*, *Sycamore Review*, and elsewhere. A native of Australia, she is based in Baton Rouge, Louisiana, where she teaches writing at Franciscan University.

Brian Blanchfield is the author, most recently, of *Proxies: Essays Near Knowing* and *A Several World* (both Nightboat). The recipient of a Whiting Award in Nonfiction and the James Laughlin Award from the Academy of American Poets, he lives in Moscow, Idaho, where he directs the MFA Creative Writing Program at the University of Idaho and teaches in the Bennington Writing Seminars.

Victoria Chang's poetry books include *OBIT*, *Barbie Chang* (both Copper Canyon), *The Boss* (McSweeney's), *Salvinia Molesta* (University of Georgia), and *Circle* (Southern Illinois University). Her children's books include *Is Mommy?* (Beach Lane), illustrated by Marla Frazee, and *Love, Love* (Sterling Children's), a middle grade novel. She lives in Los Angeles and serves as the program chair of Antioch University's low-residency MFA program.

Gillian Conoley's *A Little More Red Sun on the Human: New and Selected Poems* (Nightboat) won the Northern California Book Award. The recipient of the 2017 Shelley Memorial Award for lifetime achievement from the Poetry Society of America, she is also the translator of *Thousand Times Broken* (City Lights), a collection of three books by Henri Michaux; and poet-in-residence and professor of English at Sonoma State University where she edits *Volt*.

Miguel Coronado was the 2021 Editorial Fellow at A Public Space.

Tim Devin is a Boston artist and archivist.

Katie Foster is a writer, editor, and artist based in Omaha, Nebraska. She has worked as a bookseller at Raven Book Store in Lawrence, Kansas, and at the Lawrence Public Library. She was a 2020 A Public Space Writing Fellow.

Joshua Furst is the author, most recently, of the novel *Revolutionaries*. His previous books include *The Sabotage Cafe* and *Short People* (all Vintage).

Dagoberto Gilb is the author of *The Magic of Blood, Woodcuts of Women,* and, most recently, the story collection *Before the End, After the Beginning* (all Grove). The recipient of Whiting and Guggenheim Awards, he also edited *Hecho en Tejas: An Anthology of Texas Mexican Literature* (University of New Mexico). He lives in Austin, Texas, and Mexico City.

Huan He's poems have appeared or are forthcoming in *Beloit Poetry Journal*, *Hayden's Ferry Review*, and *Palette Poetry*. He is a PhD candidate in the Department of American Studies and Ethnicity at the University of Southern California.

Rosemarie Ho is a writer and fact-checker from Hong Kong. Her work has been published in the *Nation*, the *Outline*, and the *Point*. She is a student at the Iowa Writers' Workshop and was a 2020 A Public Space Writing Fellow.

Crawford Hunt studied linguistics at the University of Texas at Austin. After graduating, she spent a year in Chiapas, Mexico, on a Fulbright Fellowship. She lives in New York City and was a 2020 A Public Space Writing Fellow.

John Francis Istel teaches ninth grade English Language Arts at New Design High School in New York City. He lives in Brooklyn.

Corita Kent (1918–1986) was an artist, educator, and advocate for social justice.

Mi Jin Kim was born in Seoul and grew up in Los Angeles. She holds an MFA from the Helen Zell Writers' Program at the University of Michigan, where she was a recipient of the Henfield and Frederick

Busch Prizes in Fiction. Her work has appeared in *Crazyhorse*. She lives in South Korea. Her story in this issue was edited by Laura Preston.

Joanna Klink is the author of five books of poetry, most recently *The Nightfields* (Penguin). Her poems have appeared in many anthologies, including *Resistance, Rebellion, Life: 50 Poems Now* (Knopf); and *The Penguin Anthology of Twentieth Century American Poetry*. She has received awards and fellowships from the Rona Jaffe Foundation, Civitella Ranieri, the Bogliasco Foundation, the American Academy of Arts and Letters, the Trust under the will of Amy Lowell, and the John Simon Guggenheim Memorial Foundation. She teaches at the Michener Center for Writers in Austin, Texas.

Sana Krasikov is the author of the story collection *One More Year*, which was a finalist for the PEN/Hemingway Award; and the novel The Patriots (both Spiegel & Grau), which received the Prix du premier roman in France.

Sylvia Legris's most recent poetry collection is *Garden Physic* (New Directions).

Mara Faye Lethem is an award-winning translator of contemporary Catalan and Spanish prose, and the author of *A Person's A Person, No Matter How Small* (Antibookclub). Her recent translations include books by Patricio Pron, Max Besora, Javier Calvo, Marta Orriols, Toni Sala, Alicia Kopf, and Irene Solà. She is currently translating the work of Pere Calders as part of her PhD at the University of St Andrews.

Maja Lukic's work has appeared or is forthcoming in the *Adroit Journal*, *Prelude*, and *Colorado Review*. She lives in Brooklyn.

Matt Magee is an American artist best known for his abstract geometric paintings, sculptures, prints, assemblages, murals, and photographs. He lives and works in Phoenix.

Sara Majka is the author of *Cities I've Never Lived In* (A Public Space/Graywolf). She lives in Providence and teaches at the Rhode Island School of Design.

Marcelyn McNeil lives and works in Dallas. Her work has been exhibited widely across the United States, including at the San Antonio Museum of Art, the Galveston Arts Center, and the Lawndale Art Center. *Marcelyn McNeil: Works* will be published this year by Radius Books.

Matt Miller is the coeditor of *Every Hour, Every Atom: A Collection of Walt Whitman's Early Notebooks and Fragments* (University of Iowa). He is the chair of the English Department at Yeshiva University's Stern College in Manhattan, and lives in Queens.

Ron Nagle was born in San Francisco, where he currently lives and works. The sculptures and drawings in this issue were exhibited recently at Matthew Marks.

Idra Novey is a novelist, poet and translator. Her third novel, *Take What You Need,* is forthcoming from Viking. Her co-translation with Ahmad Nadalizadeh of Iranian poet Garous Abdolmalekian, *Lean Against This Late Hour* (Penguin), was a finalist for the 2020 PEN

Poetry in Translation Prize. She teaches fiction at Princeton University.

Uche Okonkwo was born and raised in Lagos, Nigeria. Her fiction has appeared in *One Story, Ploughshares, the Best American Nonrequired Reading 2019,* and *Lagos Noir* (edited by Chris Abani), among other publications. She is a 2021-2022 Steinbeck Fellow at San Jose State University and a PhD student at University of Nebraska-Lincoln.

Joan Perucho (1920-2003) was born in Barcelona. His best-known work, *Natural History* (Les històries naturals), was included in Harold Bloom's *Western Canon*. The stories in this issue are from his *Històries apòcrifes* (Apocryphal Stories).

Atsuro Riley received the Alice Fay di Castagnola Award from the Poetry Society of America for his most recent book, *Heard-Hoard* (University of Chicago). His debut collection, *Romey's Order* (University of Chicago), received the Kate Tufts Discovery Award, the Believer

CONTRIBUTORS

Poetry Award, and the Witter Bynner Award from the Library of Congress. His honors also include a Whiting Award in Poetry and a Lannan Foundation Literary Fellowship Brought up in the South Carolina low country, Riley lives in San Francisco.

Angela María Spring's work can be found in *Catapult*, *Literary Hub*, *PANK*, and elsewhere. She is the poetry editor of the *Washington Independent Review of Books* and the owner of Duende District, a mobile boutique bookstore.

Robert Sullivan's books include *My American Revolution* (FSG), *Cross Country*, and *Rats* (both Bloomsbury). He is a contributing editor at A Public Space.

Maria Thomas's fiction has appeared on BBC Radio 4, in the *New England Review*, *Wasafiri*, the *Masters Review Anthology IV*, edited by Roxane Gay, and elsewhere. She is a PhD candidate in creative writing at Goldsmiths, University of London. Her story in this issue was edited by Sarah Blakley-Cartwright.

Rebecca Wolff is the founding editor of *FENCE*. Her books include the novel *The Beginners* (Riverhead) and five poetry collections, including the forthcoming *Slight Return* (Wave).

Matthew Zapruder is the author most recently of *Father's Day*, and *Why Poetry*. He is editor at large at Wave Books, and teaches in the MFA program in creative writing at Saint Mary's College of California.

CREDITS

IMAGES

Page 3, 8, 10: Marcelyn McNeil, *Soak*, 2020, oil on canvas, 50 × 48 inches (127 × 121.92 cm); *Speed*, 2010, oil on panel, 75 × 70 inches (190.5 × 177.8 cm); and *Slow-Moving Greyscale*, 2016, oil on canvas, 52 × 54 inches (132.08 × 137.16 cm). From *Marcelyn McNeil: Works* (Radius Books, 2022). Courtesy Radius Books and the artist.

66-67: Matt Magee, *Form in Space*, 2016, twist ties, rod, marble base, 25 ½ x 11 ½ x 8 inches and Unicode, 2015–17, oil on panel, 36 x 36 inches. From *Matt Magee: Works 2012-2018* (Radius Books, 2019). Courtesy Radius Books and the artist.

94-95: Ron Nagle, *Only the Homely*, 2021, ceramic, catalyzed polyurethane, epoxy resin, and acrylic, 5 1/4 x 4 3/4 x 6 1/2 inches, 13 x 12 x 17 cm, NAGR.SC.47865. Photography: William Pruyn; *WPLJ (White Port & Lemon Juice)*, 2021, ceramic, catalyzed polyurethane, and epoxy resin, 5 x 5 x 6 1/8 inches, 13 x 13 x 16 cm, NAGR.SC.47862. y Photography: William Pruyn; and *Untitled*, 2020, ink, colored pencil, and graphite on craft paper, 10 7/8 x 8 3/8 inches, 28 x 21 cm, signed and dated in graphite (lower right recto): Nagle 2020. NAGR.DR.47908. Photography: Aaron Wax. ©Ron Nagle, courtesy Matthew Marks Gallery.

119–122: Corita Kent images courtesy of the Corita Art Center, Los Angeles, corita.org.

TEXT

131: "The Metaphor Game" was selected by Jonathan Lethem as the winner of the Academy for Teachers' 2021 Stories Out of School Flash Fiction Contest.

PATRONS

Jeremy Martin
Nancy J. Martinek
E.J. McAdams
Robert McAnulty
Julia McDaniel
Elizabeth and McKay
McFadden
Claire Messud
Jennifer R. Miller
William Morris
Judy Mowrey
Lubna Najar
Maud Newton
Elizabeth Norman
Idra Novey
Cliona O'Farrelly
Beth O'Halloran
Mo Ogrodnik
Eric Oliver
Zulma Ortiz-Fuentes
George Ow, Jr.
Danai M Paleogianni
Sandra Park
Carolie Parker
Sigrid Pauen
Perlita Payne
Samuel Perkins
Debra Pirrello
Kathryn Pritchett
Yan Pu
Kirstin Valdez Quade
Alice Quinn
Jon Quinn
Carlos Ramos
Chicu Reddy
Tina Reich
Adeena Reitberger
Mickey Revenaugh
Ann Ritchie
Susan Z. Ritz
Sarah A. Rosen
Julia Rubin
Nicole Rudick
Ruth and Kirsten
Saxton
Peter Schmader
Jill Schoolman
Fern Schroeder
Wayne Scott
Jennifer Sears-Pigliucci

Diana Senechal
Elizabeth Shepardson
Nedra Shumway
Murray Silverstein
Tina Simcich
Judy Sims
Gabrielle Howard and
Martin Skoble
Michele Smart
Adrianna Smith
Karen Smith
The Smith Family
Timothy Soldani
Sarah Soliman
Maria Soto
Peter Specker
Laura Spence-Ash
Helen Wickes and
Donald Stang
Judith Sturges
Robert and Suzanne
Sullivan
Sam Swope
Kevin Thurston
Alexander Tilney
Elizabeth Trawick
Rick Trushel
Brooke Tucker
Georgia Tucker
Charity Turner
Marina Vaysberg
Franklin Wagner
Terry Wall
Patricia Wallace
Marcia Watkins
Joyce Watts
Susan Wheeler
Katie Wilson
Mary Beth Witherup
Heather Wolf
Sierra Yit
Jenny Xie

AVAILABLE FROM A PUBLIC SPACE BOOKS

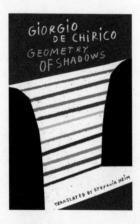

W-3: A MEMOIR
BETTE HOWLAND
Introduction by Yiyun Li

"As daring and thwarted an
American heroine as any."
—Parul Sehgal, *New York
Times*

CALM SEA AND
PROSPEROUS VOYAGE
Selected Stories
BETTE HOWLAND

"Cooler than a cocktail and
sharper than a Japanese
knife." —the *Guardian*

GEOMETRY OF
SHADOWS
GIORGIO DE CHIRICO
Translated by Stefania
Heim

"As mysterious as his
paintings." —Jhumpa Lahiri

CAPITAL
Photographs and Essay
MARK HAGE

"Each rectangle is its own
poem." —Anne Elliott

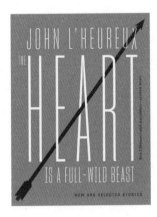

**THE HEART IS
A FULL-WILD BEAST
New and Selected Stories
JOHN L'HEUREUX**

"Capturing the deepest yearnings
of the human heart." —David
Henry Hwang

**TOLSTOY TOGETHER
85 Days of War and Peace
YIYUN LI**

"A milestone not just in reading
but in living." —Michael Langan

**THE COMMUNICATING
VESSELS
FRIEDERIKE MAYRÖCKER
Translated by Alexander
Booth**

"A raw literary meditation on
loss." —*Kirkus*

**THE BOOK OF ERRORS
Imagined Architectures
ANNIE COGGAN**

"Fact and fiction, real and
imaginary, dance in this book."
—*World-Architect*

"A CABINET OF WONDERS"*

A PUBLIC SPACE
No. 29

GERTRUDE
ABERCROMBIE
KAVEH AKBAR
LAYLAH ALI
JAMES ALLEN HALL
SELVA ALMADA
JJ AMAWORO
WILSON
KAREN AN-HWEI LEE
RUSSELL ATKINS
MARY JO BANG
ARI BANIAS
BRUCE BARBER
MEGAN BERKOBIEN
MARK BIBBINS
KAYLA BLATCHLEY
DANIEL BORZUTZKY
MARCEL
BROODTHAERS
LILY BROWN
DAVID BOYD
ANNE BOYER
JAMEL BRINKLEY
NIN BRUDERMANN
PETER BUSH
BRIAN CALVIN
LEA CARPENTER
WENDY CHEN
ANNIE COGGAN
KATE COLBY
MARGARET JULL
COSTA
GREGORY
CREWDSON
P. SCOTT
CUNNINGHAM
BRUNA DANTAS
LOBATO
KIKI DELANCEY
MÓNICA DE LA
TORRE
YOHANCA DELGADO

JILL DESIMINI
JENN DÍAZ
ALEX DIMITROV
TIMOTHY DONNELLY
ANNE ELLIOTT
EMMET ELLIOTT
ALICE ELLIOTT DARK
GRAHAM FOUST
JOHN FREEMAN
WILL FRYER
MINDY FULLILOVE
ELISA GABBERT
N. C. GERMANACOS
TEOLINDA GERSÃO
REGINALD GIBBONS
MARIA GILISSEN
CASSANDRA GILLIG
KRISTEN GLEASON
MICHAEL GOLDBERG
MATTHIAS GÖRITZ
MARILYN HACKER
MARK HAGE
KIMIKO HAHN
SARAH HALL
DAVID HAYDEN
STEFANIA HEIM
JAMIL HELLU
JORDAN JOY
HEWSON
HILDA HILST
MISHA HOEKSTRA
JENNY HOLZER
BETTE HOWLAND
TIMOTHY HURSLEY
RANA ISSA
LÍDIA JORGE
FADY JOUDAH
ALEXANDER KAN
JENA H. KIM
ROBERT KIRKBRIDE
TAISIA KITAISKAIA
JAMIL KOCHAI
JHUMPA LAHIRI
EDUARDO LALO
DAVID LARSEN
AMY LEACH
LE CORBUSIER
SUZANNE JILL LEVINE
YIYUN LI
KELLY LINK
GORDON LISH
ARVID LOGAN

BEN LOORY
MARIE LORENZ
BRIDGET LOWE
VICKI MADDEN
JORDANA MAISIE
NIKKI MALOOF
KNOX MARTIN
RANIA MATAR
MELISSA MCGRAW
PHOEBE MCILWAIN
BRIGHT
MEREDITH MCKINNEY
DEIRDRE MCNAMER
JAMES ALAN
MCPHERSON
ALEXANDER
MCQUEEN
EDWARD
MCWHINNEY
CLAIRE MESSUD
ERIKA MIHÁLYCSA
CLEO MIKUTTA
STEVEN MILLHAUSER
GOTHATAONE
MOENG
QUIM MONZÓ
INGE MORATH
SUNEELA MUBAYI
BONNIE NADZAM
DORTHE NORS
LISA OLSTEIN
CATHERINE PIERCE
TAYLOR PLIMPTON
ANZHELINA
POLONSKAYA
ALISON POWELL
JULIA POWERS
LI QINGZHAO
ANNA RABINOWITZ
PACO RABANNE
NATASHA RANDALL
NEAL RANTOUL
SRIKANTH REDDY
RICHARD ROBBINS
MERCÈ RODOREDA
MATTHEW ROHRER
SAMUEL RUTTER
SASHA SABEN
CALLAGHAN
CHERYL SAVAGEAU
DENISE SCOTT
BROWN

SCOTT SHANAHAN
AL-SHAMMAKH IBN
DIRAR
FARIS AL-SHIDYAQ
CALLIE SISKEL
EVA SPEER
THOMAS STRUTH
ROBERT SULLIVAN
CLAIRE SYLVESTER
SMITH
FIONA SZE-LORRAIN
DEBORAH TAFFA
ZSUZSA TAKÁCS
KAT THACKRAY
ERNEST THOMPSON
SYLVAN THOMSON
COLM TÓIBÍN
RICHARD TUTTLE
LYNN UMLAUF
NANOS VALAORITIS
THANASSIS
VALTINOS
MIYÓ VESTRINI
ANDREW WACHTEL ·
LATOYA WATKINS
KYLE FRANCIS
WILLIAMS
MINDY WONG
JENNY XIE
WENDY XU
LYDIA XYNOGALA
MATVEI
YANKELEVICH
YANYI
JOSEPH YOAKUM
ZHANG ZAO
ZARINA
ADA ZHANG
ELIZABETH ZUBA
...AND MORE

A PUBLIC SPACE
No. 33